"One more slight on my character and I shall..."

"What will you do?" Jay challenged as Rebecca stumbled over the fury of words. "Scream?" he taunted through cruelly smiling lips. "Who would come running but dear Olivia?"

"I hate you. I despise what you are and everything you stand for," she hissed. "And if Olivia still possesses that warped kind of view on life, then I'm sure you deserve each other! Being married to you must feed it constantly!"

He went still, and Rebecca began to quail inside, fearing that she might have gone too far. Then, "Married?" he choked. "Where the hell did you get the idea that Olivia and I are married?"

Rebecca stared at him. "You mean—you aren't?" The disbelief was clear in her voice, and Jay laughed, a harsh, cutting sound that made her wince.

"I don't need to marry Olivia to get what I want from her," he bit out scornfully. "Just as I didn't need to marry you for the same reason!"

MICHELLE REID lives in Cheshire, England, dividing her time between being a full-time housewife and mother, looking after her husband and two teenage daughters and writing. She says her family takes it very well, fending for themselves until she "comes up for air," though she's not sure which they find harder to put up with, being cleaned and polished when she's in a housekeeping mood, or being totally ignored when she's absorbed in writing and tends to forget they're alive! She has a passion for fresh air and exercise, which she gets at the local tennis club.

Books by Michelle Reid

Don't miss any of our special offers. Write to us at the following address for information on our newest releases.

Harlequin Reader Service
P.O. Box 1397, Buffalo, NY 14240
Canadian address: P.O. Box 603,
Fort Erie, Ont. L2A 5X3

MICHELLE REID

The Dark Side of Desire

Harlequin Books

TORONTO • NEW YORK • LONDON
AMSTERDAM • PARIS • SYDNEY • HAMBURG
STOCKHOLM • ATHENS • TOKYO • MILAN
MADRID • WARSAW • BUDAPEST • AUCKLAND

Harlequin Presents first edition February 1993
ISBN 0-373-11533-4

Original hardcover edition published in 1991
by Mills & Boon Limited

THE DARK SIDE OF DESIRE

CHAPTER ONE

REBECCA stood staring at the notices column in the national daily spread out in front of her. She looked pale and vulnerable all of a sudden, so brittle that there was a real chance she might break in two if anyone so much as touched her.

'W-what are you going to do?' Christina asked huskily.

It was still early morning. The day's work only just beginning. Beyond the closed door of her small front-room office Rebecca could hear the reassuring whirr of several sewing machines, interspersed with the light-hearted chatter from their five employees, discussing the local gossip of the day.

'I don't know,' she said, not moving her unblinking gaze from the column where the large black-framed box seemed to be leaping threateningly out at her:

> Will Miss Rebecca Shaw, last known to reside in the village of Thornley in South Yorkshire, please contact this telephone number urgently, as her mother is seriously ill?

'No! I won't do it! I don't know how you can even suggest it to me!'

She twisted abruptly away to stare at the grey winter view outside the office window, the echoing cries of that frightened and distraught sixteen-year-old girl ringing shrilly down the ten-year gap since they had been spoken.

It was bitterly cold outside, the cruel north wind whipping up a flurry of left-over snow, tossing it like powder into the air. A Coca-Cola can went rolling down the street, rattling against the curb, then rolling off again as the wind picked it up and ran excitedly with it, and an old woman, struggling along with her loaded shopping-basket, looked chilled to the bone.

As Rebecca stood there, her mind sent thoroughly blank, a young boy came racing around the corner on his bike, his anorak hood tied tightly around his face, his sturdy legs pumping furiously as he pedalled against the wind. She smiled, her first real smile since Christina had dumped the newspaper down in front of her. His nose was red, his blue eyes sparkling with the thrill of the battle he was having with the wind. Loving it.

'Rebecca?' The smile died, her grey eyes losing their moment of pleasure. 'She's your mother,' Christina said anxiously. 'She's ill. She must be asking for you. You can't simply ignore it.'

'You will do this, Rebecca, or I never want to set eyes on you again...!'

'No,' she murmured drily, 'I don't suppose I can.'

'I-I could ring the number for you, if you like,' Christina suggested tentatively. 'Find out just how ill she is...'

'No.' Rebecca shook her head, the dark mass of rich brown hair rustling against the collar of her soft knit jacket. She knew just who that number belonged to. Even after ten long years she could still chant it out to herself. It was the private telephone number of Thornley Hall. Jay's telephone number.

'Jay doesn't love you, you fool! He just took what you so freely gave to him! Like all men, he's only human, and you threw yourself at him all summer long!'

Rebecca swayed where she stood, the terrible pain she'd felt ten years ago battering at her soul as cruelly now as it had battered her then. She hadn't believed her mother then, of course. She had been just sixteen years old, madly—blindly—in love, and frightened. It had taken the heart-rending proof from another source to force her to accept it all. And then she had believed, every word, every hard, cruel, shaming word.

There was the muffled sound of the front door closing, then the scrape and scramble of a bike being fed into the narrow hall to lean against the side of the stairs, and Rebecca turned just in time to see the office door fly open, the windswept and reddened face of a grinning schoolboy suddenly filling the doorway. 'Hi, Mum!' he greeted her excitedly. 'Gosh, have you seen the wind out there? It almost blew me off my bike!'

Something pinched painfully at her heart, the wrenching tug of a mother's unassailable love for her only child, and she felt herself go cold inside, a fear, the like of which she had never experienced in ten eventful years, clawing its way into her soul.

'Kit,' she said quietly, 'I have to go away for a few days. Would you mind very much staying with Christina and Tom until I can get back?'

'Gosh, no!' he said, coming further into the room and bringing a waft of clean fresh air with him. 'Uncle Tom'll take me fishing if I ask him nicely.' His cheeky grin winged its way over to Christina, holding a lethal charm his mother recognised with a different kind of ache. Then he was frowning as he turned to face his mother. 'But where are you going? Not another rag-hunt, surely?' He sighed. 'I thought you'd already got your spring cloth ordered.'

Rebecca jumped eagerly on his mistake, glad he had given her an acceptable excuse. 'Yes,' she said, flashing Christina a brief but telling glance. 'Yes, I'm afraid that's it. We've just heard of a new mill up in Yorkshire that Christina thinks we should take a look at.'

'OK.' He shrugged it all aside as nothing new to him. All his life his mother had been going off and leaving him with his Aunt Christina and Uncle Tom while she hunted for good fabrics at good prices to make up her own clever designs. And they liked having him; being childless themselves and never actually likely to have a baby of their own, they enjoyed it when Kit came to stay with them.

'Seeing as it's the half-term break from school,' Christina put in brightly, 'we could perhaps take in a McDonalds and the pictures one evening, if you like.'

'Oh, great! Yes, please, Aunt Chrissy!' With a single bound he reached his surrogate aunt's side and gave her a quick hug. 'When do you have to go?' he asked his mother, bringing a rueful smile to her face at his eagerness to be rid of her.

Then the smile died, and she had to turn away so that Kit wouldn't see the sudden bleakness which entered her eyes. 'I don't know yet, but it could be right away... I have a few phone calls to make first...'

'Gosh, look at the time!' Christina said suddenly, sending Rebecca a worried glance. 'The crew will be yelling if they don't get their cup of tea soon. Come and help me, Kit,' she ordered the young boy, 'and we can make our own plans while your mother makes hers...'

Rebecca watched him go with her heart in her eyes, seeing Jay standing tall and sturdy beside Christina in the younger form of her son, so completely his double that she often found herself wondering how she could love the son so unreservedly yet despise the very thought of the man from whose loins he had sprung.

She sat down behind the desk, lowering her paste-white face into her trembling hands as the memories came crowding in. 'Hell!' she whispered thickly. 'Why couldn't they leave me alone?'

It was ten years ago that Rebecca met Jay for the first time as a woman trying desperately to blossom out of the wild and wilful child she had been. Just sixteen years old and so in love with life that it showed in the glowing beauty of her young face when Jay came looking for her that fatal summer.

He was just home from university for the last time, with his honours degree in his pocket and impatient to take up the role which had always been waiting for him at his father's side in the multi-million-pound conglomerate he ran from his Harrogate base with a rod of shrewd sharp iron.

Wealthy landowners for as far back in history as the family tree stretched, the Lorence family was considered the élite of the élite in the area. Yet, for all the differences in their social ranking, Jay had always been an important part of Rebecca's life for as long as she could remember. It was Jay who taught her how to ride her first horse, introducing her to a new and wholly absorbing way of easing her wild and restless nature in the sheer joy of galloping across the beauty of the Yorkshire countryside on one of his big powerful horses, with the wind tugging her unruly mane of russet-brown hair away from her lively face, revelling in the sheer delight of freedom the privilege gave her. A freedom from the stern restrictions of an over-critical mother, from the hurt constantly inflicted by a father who thought more of his precious roses than he did of his daughter. Of a child who, in Jay's words, was born at the wrong time in the wrong place, who should have been a gypsy rather than the daughter of a staid and disapproving housekeeper and an aloof and withdrawn gardener father.

It was always Jay who turned up when she was in trouble. Jay who dragged her choking out of the river when she was in real danger of drowning, then spanked her soundly for daring to swim in it at spring-flood time. It was Jay who held her close, rocking her gently in his arms when her father died of a sudden and unexpected heart attack. And it was Jay who shielded her from much of her mother's wrath when the need to escape the rigid chains applied to a mere housekeeper's daughter sent her whirling into one mad prank or another just for the sheer necessity of wanting to feel alive—really alive.

It was also Jay who, the year before that fatal summer, pulled her, kicking and protesting, out of Joe Tyndell's car when, at the confusing age of fifteen, she had decided it was time to experience what all her friends at school already knew—what it was like to be thoroughly kissed.

'Isn't it enough that everybody already thinks you're completely uncontrollable without them thinking you wanton as well?' he'd shouted at her, pulling, half dragging her back down the lane which led to the Hall.

'We were only kissing, for God's sake, Jay!' she'd derided him hotly, secretly appalled that Jay of all people had caught her in such an embarrassing situation. 'A girl has to learn how to some time!'

He had turned furiously on her, a man himself by then, tall and lean and excitingly handsome. There had been a full moon that night, and it shone down upon his jet-black head, bathing him in an aura of pale silver light. But it was the piercing blueness of his eyes which had held her attention as they had run in harsh condemnation over her slim, defiant frame dressed in a simple white summer blouse and wrap-around chambray skirt.

'Just look at you!' he'd sneered. 'It takes more than a kiss to get the buttons on your blouse undone!'

In horrified embarrassment she'd glanced down to find that what he was saying was true!

'You're not even wearing a bra!' he'd ground out.

'Girls don't these days,' she'd mumbled defensively, tugging the two flimsy sides of her blouse together, so full of mortification that she could no longer look at him.

'A certain kind of girl doesn't!' he'd snapped, then had taken her utterly by surprise by grasping her around her waist and pulling her hard against his lean angry body. 'If you wanted damned lessons on kissing, Becky, then you should have come to me!' he'd murmured roughly. 'After all, I've taught you everything else you know, haven't I?'

She could still remember her own stirring awareness of him as she had glanced up nervously to catch his glittering blue gaze, sensed the angry intent pulsing in him, whispered, 'No, Jay!' in a breathless little protest, then been flung into a maelstrom of new feeling when the hot sting of his mouth had come crushing down upon her own.

Nothing—nothing in all her wild adventurous fifteen years had prepared her for what happened that warm moonlit night. Not the path his anger had taken, not the kiss, not the frightening flare of passion which had erupted between them as his hands had come, warm and knowing, on to her naked breasts, stroking them, kneading them, bringing them pulsing into life in a way which had held her shocked and motionless in his arms while she had eagerly stored the new and exciting sensations.

Then he'd thrust her away from him, standing back to sear her flesh with a bitter look as she had stood there, swaying, so lost in the wonder of it all that she could barely draw in air to her heaving lungs. 'You keep away from boys, Becky!' he'd commanded raspingly. 'Do you hear? You keep damned well away from them!' Then he'd gone, striding off up the lane with quick angry strides, and by the time she'd thought to run after him he'd gone, in through the gates of the Hall, and on up the drive past the lodge house where she lived with her mother, his tall frame looking grim and unapproachable in the silver moonlight.

The next day he was gone—back to university, and they didn't lay eyes on each other for almost a year. But when Jay did eventually come upon her that next summer he found himself looking at a different Rebecca: one who had grown from child-wanton to woman, emerging from her gypsy-like chrysalis with a kind of exotic beauty which knocked him for six.

He found her by the river, sitting on a blanket, engrossed in the latest block-buster sex and crime novel
which was currently taking the world by storm. It was
a beautiful day, hot and humid, the surface of the river
barely stirring in the warm still air. She was wearing a
pair of skimpy pale blue shorts and a white vest top, her
slender arms and long shapely legs already sheened with
a light golden tan from long days of sunny weather.

She had no idea how long he'd been standing there
beneath the shade of one of the trees crowding the banks
along that part of the river, but she suddenly became
aware of being watched, and turned her head, finding
him standing there leaning against the tree, his dark face
hooded, his hands thrust into the tight pockets of his
jeans.

'Hi,' he said almost warily.

'Hi,' she replied, sending him a shy little smile. 'I heard
you were home.' An oddly intense silence held them while
she looked at him and he looked back at her. Then he
was loping over to her, his face still guarded as he
dropped down on the blanket beside her and flipped over
the cover on the book she had discarded when she saw
him.

'A bit raunchy for you, isn't it?' he remarked, reading
the title.

'Yes,' she grinned, the wicked lights alive in her clear
grey eyes. But something in his gaze had made her feel
breathless suddenly, and she had to hunt to find something light to say to him. 'Congratulations, by the way.'
She found it in remembering he had just left university.
'I believe you graduated with honours.'

His dark head bowed in wry acknowledgment. 'I am
actually allowed to be classed as a man now.' The wryness
deepened into something almost cynical, and she eyed
him with sympathetic understanding. Rebecca might
have had a hard time growing up under the restriction
placed on her own naturally impetuous nature, but in

his own way, and for all his rich and privileged lifestyle, Jay had had his problems too, trying to come up to the impossibly high standards his despotic father set for him.

'A whole summer at home...' he sighed contentedly as he stretched himself out beside her, his head resting on his bent arm so that he could watch the play of sunlight through the tree branches above them. 'Then I'm to be shipped off to America for a year, to learn the ropes from the bottom end up before being let loose on any of my father's companies.'

Rebecca looked away, a sudden bleakness clouding her lovely eyes. 'We have to grow up, I suppose,' she murmured wistfully.

'Yes,' Jay said, studying her delicate profile. 'But I think you've already started doing that.' He lifted a finger to run it lightly down the side of her smooth jaw. 'Have you been good while I've been away?'

That brought a dancing smile to her eyes. 'Oh, yes,' she confessed. 'As good as I can be anyway. I've been too busy to be anything else since my mother's found me a job—helping Mrs Lumley out at the Grange three afternoons a week.'

'The Grange?' Jay sat up, his surprise quickly overlaid with anger. 'You shouldn't be working there, Rebecca,' he snapped. 'Unlike your mother, you aren't cut out to serve other people.'

The hint of disdain for her mother's occupation straightened her spine, pride and a ready defence of what her family was setting her grey eyes flashing. 'I'm no better or worse than my mother, Jay!' she informed him coldly. 'I feel no shame in making beds or washing floors for a living!'

'Well, if you have to make beds and wash floors for a living I would rather you did them at Thornley! Not for the damned Hamers!'

'Well, isn't that kind of you?' she flared, scrabbling angrily to her knees to begin gathering her things together so she could leave, the long silken swathe of her hair falling all over her hot and angry face. 'In other words, it's all right for me to scrub *your* floors, but not anyone else's!' After all, she'd helped her mother out often enough. Had to—it was expected of the house-keeper's daughter!

'I didn't mean that!' he snapped, grabbing her by the wrist to stop her scrambling up. 'I meant.,. Hell, Becky!' he ground out, turning her around to face him and falling back so that he was glaring up at her and she glaring down at him from her kneeling position at his side. 'Olivia Hamer must be lapping it up, having you at her beck and call like that!'

'I can manage Olivia,' she said, but she looked away from him, the blow it did to her pride having Olivia wield her bitchy power over her too raw to hide.

Olivia was two years older than Becky, a beautiful snowy blonde kitten with the same privileged back-ground as Jay. But she was as jealous as hell of the special bond Rebecca and Jay had with each other, and having Rebecca under her thumb for three afternoons a week was like manna from heaven to the other girl, though Rebecca never showed—not by word or expression—how much Olivia's disdain cut into her.

His grip on her wrist had slackened, but she didn't try moving away, gazing bleakly out across the lazy stretch of river while Jay lost himself in his own brooding thoughts.

'You still don't wear a bra,' he remarked suddenly, bringing heat to her cheeks as she swung her face back to look at him.

'It's—too hot,' she defended herself, more colour in-vading her cheeks when she saw the way his sleepy fringed gaze was wandering over the soft rise and fall of her breasts beneath their thin cotton covering.

'Beautiful,' he murmured deeply, 'beautiful...' and flicked his eyes up to clash with hers. 'I haven't been able to get the beauty of your breasts out of my mind, Becky,' he told her huskily. 'Not since I saw them gleaming at me in the moonlight that night.'

'Don't, Jay...' She wanted to move away, but the tremors running beneath the surface of her skin wouldn't let her. He lifted his free hand, bringing it up to cup one high, pointed breast, weighing it delicately in his palm, his thumb moving in a light tormenting rasp across the already taut nipple. He felt her quivering response, heard her shaken intake of air, watched her soft mouth part on a shaken gasp, and lifted his dark, impassioned eyes to hers.

'Beautiful breasts. Beautiful mouth. I couldn't forget that kiss, either,' he murmured. 'And I've been waiting a whole damned year to kiss you again!'

With a tug at her imprisoned wrist he brought her tumbling down on top of him, and with no fight at all she went to him, drowning in the heated warmth of his mouth, in the passionate caresses of his hands, and there, beneath the shade of the maple tree, with the sun dappling their naked flesh and the river sliding lazily by, Jay broke the child's chrysalis open wide and let the full-blooded and passionate woman fly free.

'I'm in love with you, Becky,' he'd whispered urgently when a knowledge of what they were doing had her putting up a weak fight against him. 'I think I've always been in love with you since time began.'

And she sank, immersing herself in the fiery warmth of that declaration. Never once questioning its honesty, never once believing that Jay, of all people, could lie to her. And for the whole summer long they were virtually inseparable, snatching moments together whenever they could, meeting in secret, hugging their new-found love for each other greedily to themselves, letting no one else in. They made love anywhere they could—everywhere they could, becoming so attuned to the other's feelings that just a look or a certain smile could set the heated buzz of awareness tripping along their veins.

By the end of that summer Rebecca was almost beside herself with grief because he had to leave her to go to America for a whole year.

'It's for the best,' Jay said grimly, holding her tightly to him as though the words alone hurt him to say. 'I have to establish myself as worthy in my father's eyes before I can begin to make demands on him. And you're so young... But when I come back, I promise you, we'll be married. You and me, sweetheart, against the world!' he'd whispered in a rough, charged voice. 'We'll be invincible!'

He went away for a year, and she hadn't seen him in ten.

Rebecca came out of her tortuous journey into the past with that thought hanging bitterly in her heart. She had left Yorkshire not long after him, with his son seeded inside her, and his father's declaration etched in fire across her soul.

'Nobody blackmails this family into marriage, my girl! You say it's Jay's, but he denies it. In fact, he questions your ability to know whose child you carry, since it is a well-known fact that you're available for anyone who asks you around here!' He'd thrust a written cheque at her then, the contempt on his face overpowered only by the contempt she had felt for herself. 'You get rid of it. It isn't that difficult these days. And there's more than enough money there to pay for it! I want no scandal attached to this family. My son will marry Olivia Hamer as has always been planned, and it's either you get rid of that baby or I'll throw both you and your mother off my property—and with little chance of her ever getting another job with the reference I shall give her! As it is,' he had gone on harshly while she'd just stood there, battered by the depth of his contempt for her, 'I don't want to see you around here again. Get out, out of my sight and out of my son's life. He wants nothing to do with the likes of you!'

'You have to do as he says, Rebecca!' her mother had cried hysterically. 'I've worked here for twenty years! I'm too old to find another job—and I don't want to! Go—go away, get rid of that baby, and, for God's sake, don't ever come back! You've shamed me enough—more than enough!'

Don't ever come back . . .

Rebecca stared at the open newspaper where the printed notice now begged otherwise, and smiled a wry, bitter twist of a smile which held nothing but contempt for herself.

She should ignore the plea in that notice—just as they had all ignored her pleas ten years ago.

With a deepening of the contempt, she lifted the telephone receiver and punched in the Yorkshire code.

CHAPTER TWO

IT HAD already grown dark by the time the train pulled into the station in Harrogate. Drained by the long and tedious journey, during which she'd had nothing better to do than just sit and think, Rebecca was glad to have to stand and pull her weekend case down from the luggage rack. She still wasn't sure why she had come, or even how she felt about her mother.

The call she had made to Thornley Hall had been brief and to the point. Whoever she had spoken to was a total stranger to her—thankfully—who called herself Mrs Musgrove, and, as soon as Rebecca had announced who she was, was quite eager to give her the information she required.

Her mother was apparently in Harrogate General's intensive care unit. 'A stroke,' she was told in that gentle Yorkshire burr she hadn't heard in years and which brought an odd lump of homesickness to her throat. 'She's calling for you all the time, poor dear, and—well—I think it best if Mr Jay explains it all to you. If you will just hang on a moment I'll——'

'No!' The mere thought of having to speak to Jay made her feel sick to her stomach. 'It won't be necessary to disturb—Mr Lorence,' she said, and quickly gave details of the travelling plans before the woman could insist on her speaking to Jay again. 'So I hope to get to the hospital by teatime,' she finished briskly, then sat back heavily in her seat to tremble violently in reaction.

Answering her mother's sick-bed call was one thing— a duty if nothing else! But having to speak to the man who was the root cause of her having reached a point in her life when she had to ask herself if she wanted to

18

be bothered seeing her own mother again—ill or not—
brought the sickness clawing back in sharp dizzying
waves.

She had wanted to drive up, but the warning of bad
weather on its way convinced her against it. She had no
wish to find herself stuck in one of Yorkshire's infamous
snow blizzards out on the moors. So the train it was,
and it had been a long, wearying journey, if only because of the deep reluctance she took with her as her
companion.

'Look after yourself, Mum,' Kit had ordered. 'And
ring me when you get there. Even trains get stopped by
blizzards, you know,' he'd added sagely, sounding more
like ninety than nine.

'I'll ring the moment I reach the hotel,' she'd
promised, hugging him to her one last time before
pinning a bright smile on her face and waving him and
Tom away from the train door.

But they hadn't left the platform, not until the train
had drawn right of the station, and she could still see
them standing there in her mind's eye, Kit's tall sturdy
figure standing chest height next to Tom's round frame,
looking so poignantly like the Jay she remembered from
her early childhood that it sent a wave of helpless
yearning wafting through her for what once had been.

The train jerked, forcing her to put out a hand to
steady herself as she swayed off balance. Then there was
that final hiss of air as the brakes went on, and they
came to a shuddering stop.

Rebecca picked up her dark woollen coat and shrugged
it on. Her fingers were trembling, she noted grimly as
she fed the large black buttons into their corresponding
holes, and she took a steadying breath, pulling on her
leather gloves and making a mental check of her appearance before gathering the rest of her things together.

She knew she looked reasonably good considering the
journey and the grave reason for it. She had slipped off

to the toilet to freshen up just half an hour before they were due to arrive, combing out her long pelt of thick wavy hair before neatly pinning it up again. But those trembling fingers spoke for themselves, and she was afraid that she was more concerned about her mother than she would like to admit to herself.

Opening the compartment door, she stepped lightly down, just one of a bustle of fellow travellers all eager to reach their destination, yet standing out without her actually knowing it. Perhaps it had something to do with the wall of cool composure she wore so aloofly around herself—erected years ago, and maintained by the sheer instinct to survive no matter what. Or maybe it had a lot to do with the woman she was, tall and lithe and naturally graceful, her movements so smooth that no one looking at her—and several male heads turned to do just that—could see the kind of self-control she was having to exert upon herself.

Whatever, to the man waiting by the platform gate sighting her sent his already impassive face into total stillness, for nothing—not the years of knowing her, watching the promise of great beauty gain fruition with each passing season, nor the years of not laying eyes on her, wondering just how that beauty had taken final shape—had prepared him for what he was actually looking at now.

His jaw clenched, lips tightening across the rigid line of his teeth as he watched her reach back into the train compartment to collect her case. Then she was walking smoothly towards him, her evenly paced strides bringing her closer and closer, and his heart began accelerating, recognition of who and what she was hitting him some-where deep, deep inside.

She hadn't noticed him yet, her dark lashes lowered over the smoky grey of her eyes, her attention caught by the person walking ahead of her.

And it was all there in the slender line of her figure, in the way she moved with a smooth sensuality that was entirely inherent. The long slender length of her legs, the graceful curve of her swan-like neck, the shape of her face, small and oval and hinting at a fragility which was so utterly deceptive, and her hair, still that long thick swathe of dark, dark brown, pinned elegantly up and away in a way the old Rebecca would never have done, but there all the same, just itching to be let down.

Yes, he thought bitterly. The beauty had definitely surpassed all his wildest imaginings, leaping out to touch senses he had thought dead long ago, cutting them to the raw.

This was Rebecca, ten years on.

She reached the gate, her gloved hand going out to offer the attendant her ticket. He heard her enquire in clear light tones where the taxi rank was situated, saw her brief smile of thanks light her smoky grey eyes at the reply, then stepped forward as she cleared the gate, blocking her way.

'Hello, Rebecca,' he greeted quietly.

Lost within her own thoughts, Rebecca froze at the sound of her name being spoken by that deep, smoothly textured and jarringly familiar voice. Something fluttered inside her, the quivering remnants of an emotion long dead, and she lifted her eyes to meet with his.

For a moment she couldn't move or speak, her gaze showing her startled surprise at finding him here. He looked cold and intimidating, yet faintly guarded as he stood there staring down at her through those blue, blue eyes of his, and all she could think was, Oh, God, he's so like Kit! So like his son!

The years of bitterness swelled to a hard lump of contempt inside her. Ten years, she was thinking, and he seemed hardly touched by the passage of time. His body was still lean and hard, his hair still that jet-black pelt of silky smoothness. He still held his head at a haughty angle, stood with the calm cool ease of a superior animal. Still possessed that rare blend of might and man which had always made him so exciting to know.

And even now, with all she had experienced at his uncaring hands, she could feel the low burning drag of attraction tug at her insides, could appreciate the beautifully proportioned frame beneath the elegance of his black cashmere overcoat. His face was still the same, all strong lines and disgustingly handsome—but leaner, harder, the bones more harshly etched by a ten-year toughening of his character.

'Hello, Jay,' she managed to say at last, adding coolly, 'I didn't expect anyone to collect me.'

His hard mouth twisted, a mere slap at derisive humour before it straightened into coldness again.

'When the prodigal returns, Rebecca,' he drawled, 'it is customary to lay out the red carpet.'

'And you consider yourself a carpet, do you?' she threw back, annoyed that he'd caught her so off balance like this. In all honesty, having Jay come to meet her had been the last thing she'd have ever expected.

At that moment, and perhaps fortunately, because his blue eyes sharpened into anger at her little quip, someone jostled by them, knocking against the small weekend case she was holding in her hand, and her attention was drawn into accepting an apology from the young man before he went rushing on again, making for the taxi rank, Rebecca noted wistfully, wishing she could do the same.

'Here, give me that.' Before she had a chance to protest, Jay had reached out and taken the case from her hand. 'My car's in the car park; it's only a short walk from here.' And with that he turned abruptly on one heel and began walking away.

Rebecca watched him go, a hand going up to clutch at the front of her warm woollen coat, her eyes fixed and unblinking on that smoothly moving frame. No, she confirmed her earlier impression, he hadn't changed much over the years. Still the same arrogance, the same blithe manner of superiority. Stepping in, taking over, taking over like some autocratic despot coming to collect the recalcitrant child!

He was already crossing the car park by the time she reached the station exit, threading his way through the rows of parked cars with the irritating certainty that she would be following behind him like some pet dog . . . no, she altered that: *whipped* dog was more like it. That last slicing glance he had given her before strolling away had told her well enough that her animosity towards him was no less passionate than his for her.

She set off after him, her slender heels clicking on the hard tarmacadam surface. By the time she reached him he had already stashed her suitcase away in the boot of some low-slung roaring thing of a car, and was waiting impatiently by the passenger door for her to join him.

She did so with a hint of her old defiance running in her veins. He had no right to treat her like a piece of unwanted but necessary baggage! She hadn't asked him to meet her train! She hadn't asked him for anything— not anything—cver!

At the door she paused for a moment to breathe in the cool winter air. It tasted clean and fresh, sharp on her lungs, with the warning of snow to come. She thought she would have forgotten, but she hadn't; there was something innately stirring in breathing in her first real lungful of Yorkshire air, and already she had slipped back into that old childish habit of savouring its clear sweet scent. Summer or winter, she had used to do it; run outside just so she could breathe it in, enjoy it, offer herself to it—love it.

'You'll freeze to death if you stand around out here much longer.'

'Sorry.' She sent him a cool glance, deliberately ignoring the critical note in his voice. This was her first visit home in ten long years. She had gone away because of him, stayed away because of him, and if he thought he was going to spoil this first burst of pleasure she'd experienced at actually being here then he could...

She got into the car, folding her slender frame into the low-slung bucket seat, picking up the distinctive smell of real leather, the air of luxury and comfort, and smiled thinly to herself as he closed the door and strode around the long car bonnet to get in beside her.

'How is my mother?' She asked the question uppermost in her mind.

Jay set the car in motion and manoeuvred them out of the parking spot before replying. 'I thought you'd never ask,' he drawled derisively.

'It was a matter of being given the chance,' she pointed out, flashing him a cold glance. Even in profile, he still looked fantastic: rich, privileged, dauntingly sophisticated.

'She's just about holding her own,' he informed her flatly.

'Tell me what happened.' She shifted her gaze frontwards, not wanting to look at him. He was obsessing her mind too much, taking it away from the problems it should be thinking about.

'She hasn't been well for some months,' he told her, steering them out on to the main road and into the steady stream of commuter traffic in the elegant spa town. 'And we were concerned enough to try to get her to ease up a bit. But you probably remember what she's like——' a faint but rueful smile touched his thin lips '—she kept on insisting she was quite well; well enough to do her job to her usual high standards.'

'Of course,' she murmured cynically. The Lorences had always come first with her mother. Even before her own daughter——

'Because she felt more useful that way!' Jay snapped out harshly, picking up on her tone and flashing her a hard look. 'She had little else to live for, did she?'

'Did I say otherwise?' she drawled, sounding bored with it all.

'No,' he clipped, 'but you implied it, though God knows what right you have to criticise when you'd forgotten you even had a mother for the last ten years!'

True, she thought, not willing to get on to that particular treadmill. She had forgotten by necessity. It was the only way she could survive those first few wretched years.

'She suffered a small stroke,' Jay went on after a short tense moment. 'Not anything too drastic in itself, but she happened to be on her way up the stairs at the Hall when it struck her, and she fell down them; broke her hip, I'm afraid. Then, on top of all that, she developed pneumonia—not an unusual complication apparently with cases like your mother's. Anyway, to cut a long story short, she's been calling for you, agitated about something, desperate to see you—to tell you something, she keeps saying. Hence the notice in the nationals— since we had no other means of finding out where you were,' he concluded deridingly.

'How long—how long has she been ill?' It was something that he had said that alerted her to the idea that all this had not taken place recently.

'A month,' he stunned her by saying. 'The stroke put a delay on their being able to treat the hip, and the delay in treating the hip brought on the pneumonia—a vicious circle,' he concluded heavily.

'Does she know I'm coming?' she asked him huskily, at last beginning to feel some aching emotion for her mother's plight. She must be hating being so ill! Hating the immobility and the feeling of uselessness. She'd always been so strong, so healthy! Never caught so much as a cold as far as Rebecca could remember.

'No,' Jay replied. 'I thought it best not to build her hopes up. Just in case you changed your mind at the last minute and decided not to bother.'

'You don't have to use the sarcasm, Jay,' Rebecca threw back wearily. 'I know exactly what you think of me without it.'

'And don't care much, by your tone.'

'No,' she flatly agreed. 'You're right, I don't care much. I've booked myself a room at the Swan——' she changed the subject '—but I would prefer to go straight to the hospital if you don't mind.'

'Not at all,' he murmured easily enough. 'But you won't be staying at the Swan. You'll be coming back to the Hall with me.'

'No way!' she gasped, horrified by the mere idea of it. With Olivia there? His father? 'No, Jay,' she bluntly refused. 'I prefer to stay at the Swan. It's closer to the hospital, and I have no desire to be more of an inconvenience to you than I have to be.'

'You've always been an inconvenience,' he grimaced, and for once didn't sound cutting, but simply rueful instead. 'I decided years ago that it was to be my karma to have Rebecca Shaw as the inconvenience of my life.'

She smiled, unable to stop herself; that quirky sense of humour of his had always managed to touch an answering chord in her own. 'Well, you've had a ten-year respite at any rate,' she threw back drily.

'Who said?' he challenged, and suddenly the air inside the car became too thick to breathe. The husky note in his voice, the way he flashed her a dark blue look told her that he was serious, deadly serious.

Conscience? she wondered, and smiled bitterly to herself as she turned her face away from him. She could still remember the ruthless way his father had delivered Jay's cruel message to her which cut him free of his promises to her in crisp clean slices from his uncaring blade.

'We're here,' he said beside her.

'Good,' she clipped, bringing his head swinging sharply around at the icy tone back in her voice. 'If you don't mind I would rather go in alone,' she told him, and scrambled out of the car the moment he brought it to a stop outside the brightly lit hospital entrance.

It had that distinctive hospital smell of antiseptic and illness, and her stomach knotted into a tight ball, her footsteps silenced by the thick-cushioned, highly polished linoleum floor-surface as she walked over to the small glass-fronted Reception desk.

'Intensive care unit, please,' she asked the porter.

'Ah, yes, miss.' He directed her with a grave smile which suited the grave place she was about to visit. 'You do have permission to go up there, don't you?' he added questioningly.

'Yes,' she said, having no idea if she had permission or not—nor caring. 'My mother is there.'

He directed her to the bank of lifts, and she moved off, shivering a little despite the controlled warmth of the place, what little colour she'd had in her face leaving her altogether as she found herself coming closer and closer to having to face her mother.

Yet still the conflict of emotions went on inside her: resentments, bitterness, born of a pride that wanted to adhere to the rules by which she had left Yorkshire ten years ago. And that terrible knot of anguish which had brought her racing up here on the first available train.

The lift doors opened and she stepped inside, turning to press the number on the indicator panel as the porter had instructed her. There was no sign of Jay in the brightly lit Reception, she noted as the doors slid shut on her. He had taken her at her word and left her alone to meet this next trauma.

She whirred upwards, small white teeth gnawing unknowingly at her full bottom lip. The doors opened, and she stepped out into a long wide corridor stretching off to her right, painted in the same blank grey paint she had encountered downstairs. And the silence here was suffocating.

There was a Reception desk further along, with a white-capped nurse sitting working at it, and she forced herself to move forward, barely seeming to disturb the mood of quiet gravity.

Then suddenly she was stopping dead in her tracks, her heart tumbling to her stomach to lie there pumping sickeningly. What she had thought was a long corridor in actual fact had suddenly opened out into a huge square room of plated glass around the nurse's desk. And behind each pane of observation glass was a bed, its poor unfortunate occupant surrounded with wires and machines giving off those nerve-tingling bleeps and hisses which said life was barely being preserved here.

Then she swayed, a pale hand going up to her clammy brow as a sudden dizziness assailed her, horror—the like of which she had never experienced in her life before— holding her trapped and rooted to the spot.

She hadn't needed to ask further where her mother's bed was, because Rebecca knew she was looking at it, looking at the frail old woman lying so grey and still behind the wall of glass, lying there as if the life was being slowly sucked out of her.

'Here, I have you.' That deep voice came quietly behind her, a hand firm and supportive on her waist, and she turned opaque eyes up to meet blankly with Jay's, then sank heavily into his arms.

CHAPTER THREE

REBECCA came round to find herself lying on a narrow vinyl couch. Jay was squatting beside her, his large hands trying to rub some warmth back into her own.

'It was a shock,' he was grimly explaining to someone—the nurse probably—who was standing behind her, applying a cool compress to her brow. 'She's only just found out her mother is ill, and she's rushed up here as soon as she could. Coming into the heat in here after the cold outside must have sent her sickly.'

'I didn't expect to just see her like that,' Rebecca whispered threadedly, bringing Jay's piercing blue eyes flickering down to meet hers. He looked pale and grim, his age at last. And she smiled at that last thought because she knew she probably looked her age, too, right now.

'I wanted to warn you, but you rushed off too quickly,' he said, then grimaced.

'Your mother is sleeping at the moment, Miss Shaw,' a soft gentle voice inserted, and the hand on her brow lifted away, so Rebecca automatically replaced her own over the cool cloth still lying here. 'So you have plenty of time to rest here and recover before you see her. I'll just go and make you a cup of tea,' the nurse offered, coming into Rebecca's vision, her thin wiry frame looking too fragile to be doing the heavy job she had made her life's work. 'Milk—sugar?' she asked smilingly.

'Yes, to both,' Jay answered for her, catching her sharp glance of protest and adding grimly, 'You need it, strong and sweet,' he prescribed.

The nurse moved away so silently that Rebecca found herself wondering fancifully if the people who worked here were soundproofed along with the floors. Then she remembered, and closed her eyes, the sickness cloying at her shocked stomach again. 'She looks so old, Jay,' she whispered unsteadily, 'so—old...'

'What do you expect after ten years?' he bit out gruffly, the angry tone making her glance sharply at him. He was looking at her as though he despised her. The hard line of his mouth turned downwards and thin. He flashed her a cold blue look. 'She's in here because of you, Rebecca,' he accused coldly. 'She's in here because you walked away and left her with nothing but the Hall and us to care whether she lived or died! So don't expect me to offer you sympathy because fate has caught up with you at last!' He stood up, his long body tight, then the blue eyes were cutting into her again. 'The only time she felt life was worth living over these last ten years was when she was working flat out for us!'

'But that's always been true!' she threw back defensively, pushing herself into a sitting position, then closing her eyes as another wave of dizziness swept over her. 'Your home and your family always came before me, Jay—and don't try denying it, because you above all people know it's the truth.'

Silence fell by mutual agreement, the time nor the place the right one for this kind of discussion. Rebecca kept her face hidden in her hand, and Jay stood stiffly beside her, those awful rhythmic bleeps and hisses the only thing breaking the angry silence.

'Here,' a gentle voice said, sounding like a breath of fresh air after the hard aggression in Jay's. 'This will make you feel better.' Rebecca lifted her face to find the nurse standing there offering her a cup and saucer. Her stomach lurched, but she took it, smiling a wan thanks. 'Take your time and drink your tea,' she advised, 'and by then your mother should be waking up.'

'She's not in a coma, then?' Rebecca asked, her heart leaping to grab at this small piece of hope.

'No.' The nurse placed a reassuring hand on her shoulder. 'Just sleeping. The worst, we hope, is over,' she told her quietly. 'The hip is healing nicely and the fever is gone. All she needs now, to make sure of a good recovery, is to see you. She's been fretting so much—worrying about you...'

One of the beeps went out of rhythm, and the nurse lifted her head, the smile leaving her pretty round face to make way for sharp alertness. 'Excuse me,' she said, and rushed off.

Rebecca watched her go, scurrying silently towards a room on the other side of the ward. No doors to push through, just the plate-glass windows and a gap, which she rushed through to the poor faceless person lying in the bed.

'God,' Jay muttered suddenly, 'I couldn't work in here. I couldn't take the stress of it.'

'No,' Rebecca agreed, grimacing as she put down the cup and saucer, then slowly she asked, 'Jay...why didn't you try to make contact with me when my mother was at her worst?'

He didn't look at her, his attention seemingly fixed on the nurse who was bending concernedly over her patient. 'To be honest,' he said after a moment, 'it never entered my head. You've been gone ten years without even a word to tell us if you were alive or dead. I came to the conclusion a long time ago that you mustn't care.'

Which was the truth, she acknowledged grimly to herself. She hadn't cared, not if any of them lived or died. But she did care now, she realised as her eyes strayed over to the glass partition where her mother lay, and a feeling of fierce anguish gripped her queasy stomach.

'It was only when Lina began asking for you that I realised that she must have never given up hope of seeing you again—poor fool.' He flashed her another of those bitter looks. 'They say that there is nothing more resilient than a mother's love,' he concluded derisively.

Rebecca hooded her eyes, her thoughts winging away to a little boy safe at home with her closest friends. 'And a father's love?' she asked drily. 'How resilient is that, do you think?'

Jay was puzzled by the remark, by the bitterness which came with it, a frown creasing his high tanned brow. 'Your father may have been a quiet and withdrawn man, Rebecca, but even you can't say he didn't love you.'

She smiled at his complete misunderstanding of her words, her legs still shaky but able to support her at last. 'I'm ready to see my mother now,' she told him quietly.

Jay hesitated, looking at her oddly. But then he saw the mask of withdrawal on her face and nodded grimly, taking her arm in a firm grip which Rebecca didn't try to break. She found she needed his support right now.

'She's very weak,' he warned as they moved slowly towards her mother's room. 'And I'm afraid the stroke has left her with one side of her face slightly askew. She tends to ramble a lot, so if you can it would be best if you pretend to understand what she's talking about rather than question her, because it only further agitates her.'

She nodded, swallowing as they came to the threshold of the room. The hospital bed was cranked up high, with cot-like supports at either side. Her mother lay perfectly still, her eyes closed, looking so frail and wasted that tears filled Rebecca's eyes. Gone was the head of warm brown hair she remembered, and in its place were soft silver curls which only increased the appearance of age. Her face had hollowed, the once strong and uncompromising shape withered and pale. And her eyes were ringed by the dark blue circles of one who had been fighting a battle with herself—with life itself.

Shrugging Jay aside, she walked slowly forward until she was standing by her mother's shoulder, the swim of tears making it impossible for her to see clearly. 'Mummy?' she murmured thickly, the word quavering from her trembling lips as she waited achingly for a response.

The soft lashes flickered, fluttering against the hollowed casements of her eyes before lifting slowly, heavily, and Rebecca felt something wrench inside when she found herself gazing into the dull grey irises which had once been the same vibrant grey as her own.

'Becky...?' her breathless voice whispered disbelievingly, and a thin limp hand began scrambling across the bedclothes in an agitated effort to reach her. 'Oh, Becky.' Tears swam up to fill her eyes. 'Is it really you?'

Rebecca turned anxiously to look for Jay. He was standing at the bottom of the bed, watching with his face wiped clean of everything but grimness. 'C-can this be m-moved away?' she asked him thickly, gripping the side-panel to the bed, wanting to, *needing* to get closer to her mother so she could just hold her—hold her as she would hold Kit if he was ill or upset.

'Let me.' Jay came to her side, deftly lowering the tubular frame downwards.

'Jay...?' Her mother saw him, her weak smile accompanied by another well of helpless tears. 'You found her. You found my Becky for me.'

'Yes, Lina,' he answered gently, reaching out to brush a caring hand across the old lady's cheek. 'I found her.'

'Becky...' The watery gaze searched around Jay for her daughter again, the hunger in her eyes wrenching at Rebecca's heart. 'Oh, Jay, look how beautiful she is— so sweet...' Her hand came out towards her daughter, and Jay moved quietly aside, allowing Rebecca to take his place again, and she took her mother's hand in her own, allowing her to pull her down on the edge of the bed, letting herself be looked over as though she were some strange phenomenon likely to disappear as unexpectedly as she had arrived. 'You still have your lovely

hair, and that wonderful skin...' The eyes moved restlessly over her while Rebecca sat taking in the full
horrifying force of her mother's decline. 'You're not
smiling,' she was informed. 'You used to smile such a
lot—all the time, no matter what I...' The words
withered and died on a thickened gulp, and the tears
welled up again.

'Don't cry,' Rebecca pleaded thickly, close to tears
herself, and she reached out to cup the withered cheek
with a hand.

'I didn't think you would come,' her mother sobbed
weakly. 'I didn't think I would ever see you again!'

'Well, I'm here now,' Rebecca tremulously assured her.
'And now all you have to do is stop worrying and help
make yourself better.'

'Yes,' her mother sighed, her body going limp as she
sank back into the mound of pillows, her eyes closing,
her breathing shallow, the trace of tears glistening on
her hollowed cheeks. 'Becky...' she whispered slurringly,
struggling against the folds of sleep while the thin hand
still gripped firmly on to her daughter's, 'don't go away,
will you? I have so much I want to say to you...make
amends...no excuse...life is precious...I was
frightened...'

'Ssh,' soothed Rebecca, concerned by the agitation in
her mother's disjointed speech. 'Stop worrying yourself
over it all. It's all over now.'

A hand coming down on Rebecca's shoulder told her
what she had already recognised—that her mother was
being dragged back down into sleep, the well of emotion
draining her quickly. Too quickly for a woman who had
lived by such undaunting strength.

'Let her rest now, Rebecca,' Jay gently advised. 'Five
minutes is always only as much as she can take in one
visit. We'll come back tomorrow.'

'Jay...?' The thready sound from the bed brought
both sets of eyes on to her.

'Yes, I'm here, Lina,' he answered softly.

A frail smile touched her mother's mouth. 'Look after my Becky for me until I can get out of here. Look after her like you used to do...'

Something cruel wrenched inside Rebecca, and she stood up jerkily, shrugging his resting hand away, the old bitterness jarring its way through her body. 'I can look after myself now, Mummy,' she informed the sick woman in a cool clear voice. 'I'm all grown up now, remember.'

'Still,' Jay put in quickly, sending her a warning glare, 'Rebecca will be staying at the Hall, Lina, so you don't have to worry about her at all.'

'Bring her back tomorrow,' he was ordered.

'Yes, ma'am,' he grinned, and Rebecca found herself resenting the look of fond mischief which stretched her mother's lopsided mouth. In all her young days she could not remember her ever smiling at her quite like that. But then, she remembered cynically, her mother always had been vulnerable to Jay's easy charm.

So were you, a small voice taunted inside her head.

Reaction set in once she was out in the corridor again, and she began to shiver. Seeing her mother looking so sick and vulnerable had come as a terrible shock, the ageing process something she hadn't even thought about on her long journey up here.

'Thank you,' Jay murmured as he joined her.

'What for?' She flicked him a resentful glance. 'She's my mother. I suppose it should be me thanking you for taking the trouble to look after her.'

'Well, it's something that you recognise the fact, I suppose,' he threw back coldly.

Rebecca turned abruptly and walked off towards the lifts, the cutting reply which sprang readily to her lips in retaliation for that one severely curtailed. The fact that she had been loving and caring for his son for the

last ten years was something she had no wish to inform
him of!

'Rebecca...' His hand came to rest on her arm, and
she jerked violently away from him.

'Don't touch me!' she ground out huskily. And he
took a startled step back at the depth of hatred he saw
in her flashing eyes, thoughts of Kit and what he had
been deprived of putting it there. 'Just—don't—touch
me,' she repeated thickly, shaken so badly by the sudden
rise of bitterness that it was impossible to conceal it.

They travelled down together, Jay standing in grim
silence at her side. Outside in the cold crisp air Rebecca
paused to suck in a deep lungful of it, trying to calm
herself, steady the war of emotions going on inside her.

Jay watched her inscrutably for a moment, then turned
away. 'I'll get the car. Wait here,' he said, and she waited;
like someone's obedient dog, she waited, the cold striking
at her body, her exposed ears, the small straight tip of
her nose, without her being aware of it.

The low black sports car drew up beside her, and Jay
leaned over to open the door so that she could climb
inside. She did so without a word, and without a word
he reached across her and fastened her seat-belt, then
put the car into gear and moved away.

'I need to get to a telephone,' she said suddenly, remembering her promise to Kit and realising that he would
be starting to worry about her by now.

'You can use the one at the Hall,' Jay offered. 'It's
only twenty minutes away.'

'I don't want to stay at the Hall,' she reminded him
stubbornly. 'If you still refuse to let me stay at the Swan
then I'll use my old room at the lodge house.'

'No can do, I'm afraid.' He threaded them back into
the lighter stream of traffic and surged away, sending
her pressing back into her seat, the sensation of power
disturbing her insides. 'The Lodge is uninhabitable at
the moment. With your mother in hospital, we took the

opportunity to renovate the old place. It's a mass of scaffolding at the moment.'

'Then it will have to be the Swan,' she insisted.

'You will damn well stay at the Hall!' he bit out angrily, making her jump. He sent her a look of dislike. 'Your mother expects it, and we would look damned bad if we didn't put you up, so stop arguing about it, will you, and at least try to accept the offer graciously?'

'With suitable deference, you mean,' she scorned. 'The lowly housekeeper's daughter offering grateful thanks to the lordly Lorences?'

'That wasn't even funny,' he derided her skitting tone, 'and an insult to the way you grew up with us, Rebecca. Because I can't remember a single moment when you were made to feel inferior to me or my family.'

'How is your father?' she asked him, bringing his face around sharply to stare at her.

'Didn't you know?' he said in genuine surprise, then added drily, 'of course, you wouldn't, would you, since you've been so very careful not to contact anyone in Thornley since you left us?' He turned his face back to the road, his manner roughening slightly as he told her, 'My father died several years ago.'

Cedric Lorence—dead? 'I'm—sorry.' The word stuck, and she had a feeling Jay knew it because his mouth thinned into a hard line. 'So you're the kingpin of the Lorence empire now, are you?' she added with another slicing cut at him and all he stood for.

The remark forced an icy silence between them for the rest of the journey. And Rebecca was glad of it; she had no wish to open a line of communication with Jay, no matter how bitter a line it would be. He was a ghost from her past, and one she refused to let haunt the present. So she turned her attention to reacquainting herself with the familiar scenery beyond the car as Jay took them sweeping out of the town and on to the narrow winding country lanes which would lead them to his home.

Ten years, she mused as they drove through the tiny picturesque village of Thornley where she had lived throughout her childhood. Nothing seemed to have changed—nothing but herself.

He was telling the truth about the Lodge, she noted as they drove through the wide, open gates of Thornley Hall. It was shrouded in scaffolding, the roof gutted, and the grey stone-lintelled windows bare of glass. It looked grim and derelict in the cold dark of the night, the tall old trees half circling it bleak and barren.

She shivered, remembering the last summer she had spent there. Loving Jay, jealous of him, of any time he spent away from her, of the things she was prohibited from sharing with him which proved Jay's claims to equality an outright lie.

She could still remember the hurt and jealous resentment when she had used to watch him—hidden behind the curtains in her tiny bedroom window—drive out of those gates dressed to kill in full tuxedo, going off to attend one formal function or another. 'In place of my father,' he had used to dismiss it, not seeing how deeply it used to hurt her to know she wasn't acceptable as his companion. Those were the nights when he used to take Olivia instead. She was more than acceptable, a golden-haired princess while Rebecca was just the tousle-headed peasant.

Olivia... Thoughts of Olivia brought her eyes flicking forward to stare at the looming grandeur of Thornley Hall, its sturdy walls of local grey stone as cold and unwelcoming to her as they had always been.

There had been a Lorence in residence here since it had been built, the family tree stretching way back into Yorkshire history, and it was a beautifully preserved and enviable place to live, with the Lorence name coveted by the other wealthy in the area.

Had he married Olivia? she wondered. She hadn't thought to ask, had cast the other girl's place in Jay's life aside while she'd concentrated on her mother's plight. Feeling suddenly chill inside, she shifted her gaze to Jay, staring at the strong hands resting on the steering-wheel, his fingers long and lean, lightly peppered with fine black hair.

No damning wedding-ring glinted back at her. But that didn't mean much. Jay had always scorned such obvious things as jewellery. Even his wrist-watches had always been plain and unostentatious, though expensive, leather-strapped and plain black-faced.

The house had been settled for the cold winter night, she noted as she turned back to it, the long Georgian framed sash windows warmly draped with thickly lined velvet.

Her hands twisted tensely together on her lap, her mind busily searching for the composure it was going to need to face Olivia in the one role she had always wanted above anything else: mistress of Thornley Hall.

That last summer here had been an eye-opener in many ways for Rebecca. It was the summer she became a woman at Jay's passionate nurturing. It was also the summer she learned the bitter truth of where the dividing lines were set between working class and gentry—and not only at the ruthless hands of Jay and his father: Olivia had played a strong part too, taking great delight in stamping Rebecca's servile capacity in the world when she ordered her around like a personal slave on the three afternoons a week she worked at the Grange.

It was because of those afternoons that she and Jay had their first big row, the argument which sent her off in defiant revolt against his domination over her, sexual and otherwise.

'If you think it's all right to sit lazing around Olivia's pool flirting with her while I do her dirty washing—then it's all right for me to slum it with my friends!' she yelled at him, facing him across their special clearing down by the river, her slender figure arched forwards in usual spitting fury.

'I don't flirt with Olivia!' he denied hotly. 'I go there because I know you'll be there!'

'Liar!' she accused. 'Do you think I don't see the way you're always touching her, smiling at her—teasing her?'

'She touches me!' He scowled. 'Not the other way around.'

'Then don't let her!'

'Stop being silly, Becky,' he sighed, changing from anger to cajoling when he saw the argument getting him nowhere. It wasn't a new one; all summer long Olivia had been forcing down Rebecca's throat the social differences between them, and her pride alone would not take it lying down. 'You know I worship the ground you walk on.'

'But not enough to take *me* to the country club ball,' she denounced. 'Not enough to show them all that *I'm* the one you want to be with!'

'It isn't that simple, and you know it.' He shifted uncomfortably where he stood, his blue gaze dropping away from hers. 'You know how old-fashioned my father is. And your mother for that matter—God damn it, Rebecca, you're only sixteen!' he grated. 'They'd all lynch me if they knew what I'd allowed to happen between us!'

'Perhaps you deserve it,' she snapped, hating him because she knew there was a lot of truth in what he was saying. He was twenty-three, and should have known better than to seduce the housekeeper's sixteen-year-old daughter! Her chin came up—she could still remember now the pride with which she made the gesture. 'Well, go and take Olivia. Pretend you're the nice clean obedient boy they all believe you to be—but don't expect me to sit biting my nails at home while you do it! There are plenty of other fish in the sea besides you, Jason Lorence!'

'Go out with anyone else and I'll kill you, Becky!' he warned, and a shiver of excitement ran through her because she knew he meant it. Her grey eyes flashed in challenge, his darkened into angry threat, and she smiled, a slow, taunting, provoking little smile, and said lightly, 'What's sauce for the goose——'

'I mean it!' He began stalking her dangerously.

'So do I,' she threw back silkily, beginning to enjoy the fight. 'There's a dance on at the Black Bull tonight. Joe wants to take me.'

'Go and I'll kill him, too!' he growled.

'Go with Olivia tonight, and I'll go with Joe.'

He did, and so did she. And even now, ten years later, she still wasn't sure which of them had won that particularly bitter battle. Perhaps she had, because Jay had driven in through the Lodge gates just as Joe was kissing her goodnight, and his jealous rage alone had been worth the defiance. But maybe he had, because that was the first time he had called her a slut and a cheap little tart. And it was the first time she began to see, though she refused to accept it then, that that was exactly how Jay did see her—as nothing more than a wildly exciting, utterly desirable tart.

The tyres crunched as they came to a stop, and Rebecca blinked herself back into focus. There was another car parked in front of them, a neat little Porsche, gleaming bright red in the headlights from Jay's car.

'Hell,' he muttered tightly. 'Olivia. I'd forgotten all about her.'

As he spoke and Rebecca stiffened the front door to the Hall came open, the spill of light flooding out to where they sat, and their two heads turned to stare in silent if grim appreciation at Olivia, still lithe and slender, her golden hair haloed by the light from behind, her pale blue pure silk dress moulding her body like a second skin, her smile wide and warm and sure of its welcome.

The perfect wife, welcoming her weary husband home.

CHAPTER FOUR

'JAY, darling, at last!' Olivia went into his arms like one who belonged there, and Jay accepted the intimate warmth of her embrace while Rebecca remained inside the car, watching it all with her heart turned to stone in her breast.

This, she was thinking bitterly, was what his father was prepared to kill his unborn grandson for. To have these two people safely joined together in this house. Utter disparagement held her stiff and still as she watched them, giving them their few moments' privacy before she opened the car door and climbed slowly out.

It was Jay who broke away, half turning in the possessive crook of Olivia's arm to search Rebecca out, his gaze clashing with hers with a cold kind of triumph. Then Olivia saw her, and her blue eyes widened into incredulous surprise.

'Well,' she drawled, not moving from Jay's side, 'if it isn't little Becky Shaw.'

'Hello, Olivia,' she said flatly.

Jay released himself to come back to the car, and Olivia followed for a couple of steps, shivering as the cold air hit her uncovered arms. 'You've been to see your mother, no doubt,' she assumed, her gaze curious and faintly contemptuous on Rebecca's impassive face. 'We've all been so concerned about her, poor thing, though Jay has been marvellous with her, haven't you, darling?'

He didn't reply, his head deep inside the boot of the car.

'And Mrs Musgrove has been such a rare find, so your mother's illness hasn't managed to cause too much inconvenience here at the Hall——'

'Get in, Olivia, it's too cold to be standing out here in that flimsy dress,' Jay cut in grimly, closing the car boot with a controlled slam.

'Yes, it is chilly, isn't it?' Either not hearing, or refusing to acknowledge the warning note in his voice, Olivia smiled sweetly at him as he walked back towards the house with Rebecca's suitcase in his hand, then wound her arm into his free one, and walked in with him.

Rebecca followed at a slower pace, schooling her face, keeping a rigid control on the new set of emotions beginning to clamour inside her—all of them bitter.

Very little had changed here, was the first conscious note she made. Jay's home was inherently beautiful, a place where Lorences had resided for centuries, building on and caring for the wonderful collection of treasures they had accumulated over the years. The wide square hallway was made warm and alive by the rich gleam of fine oak panelling, the polished floor still a scatter of priceless Indian rugs. Portraits of long-deceased family members still lined the wall which took a graceful curving line up the wide sweeping staircase, and the requisite suit of armour still stood guard outside the library door.

'I expected you back ages ago,' Olivia was gently scolding Jay. 'I had to get Mrs Musgrove to put dinner back. I hope it hasn't spoiled the grouse...'

'Jay...' Quietly and coolly, Rebecca demanded his attention, watching the smooth way he extricated himself from Olivia's clinging grasp so that he could turn, her case still gripped firmly in his hand. 'I have to make that phone call,' she reminded him.

'Of course.' Putting the case down by the stairway, he strode off towards his study. 'In here,' he said, holding the door open for her.

She followed, nodding her thanks as she went to pass by him, aware of Olivia's assessing gaze on her as she moved. The room was, again, just as she remembered it, all warmth and polished wood, lined with priceless books, its only concession to the modern era the stack of technical computerised equipment she could see standing behind the wide oak desk. She noticed that the fire was lit, casting tall shadows across the elegant walls, and, as she stepped further inside, the door closed quietly behind her on the clear easy tones of Olivia's offering to mix Jay a drink.

Rebecca stood for a moment, absorbing the silence, shoulders sagging beneath her warm woollen coat, the impervious mask dropping away to show the lines of strain and emotional exhaustion it had been hiding.

Then slowly she straightened, head coming up on a controlled intake of air, as if she was having to brace herself. Her eyes flickered back into life, and, with the brisk efficiency her son would know her better for, she shrugged out of her coat and laid it across the back of one of the winged leather chairs which had stood for years flanking the big oak carved fireplace, revealing the neat elegant lines of a simple navy blue day-dress, designed and created by her own deft hands.

Then she walked over to the desk to lift the telephone receiver and dial the number which would connect her with the most important person in her world.

'Hi, Mum!' He didn't even give her a chance to say anything, and Rebecca grinned, relaxing for the first time in God knew how many hours. 'I knew it had to be you! Why has it taken you so long to call me?' he demanded.

'Hello, darling.' Her voice dropped into its usual easy tenderness, the smile on her face wiping away all her present worries. 'It's been hectic up here,' she said with a wry stab at honesty. 'And this is the first moment I've had to reach for a phone. How are you? Missing me yet?'

'Not yet,' he lied blithely.

It was a game they played: he always said the opposite to what he really meant, and she always answered it in the same way: 'Good, because I'm not missing you either!' Then they both fell into companionable laughter, belying every word.

'Hey—can you believe this?—Uncle Tom is taking me ice-skating the day after tomorrow! He reckons he's a dab hand at it—which I have got to see,' drawled her unconvinced son.

'Well, don't break a leg,' Rebecca warned drily. 'I don't fancy the idea of tripping up on your crutches all over the place.'

Behind her the study door opened. But Rebecca didn't hear it; she was too engrossed in the balming quality of her son's light chatter.

'But tomorrow we're going to the cinema,' he rushed on excitedly. 'Followed by a pizza—by triple mutual consent,' he added importantly, obviously a new saying for him, from the way he used it. 'Or, to be more honest, by my suggestion and Aunt Chrissy's sigh of relief—did you know she can't stand hamburgers?' he cried, aghast. 'She certainly never let it drop before!'

Rebecca laughed, the husky sound vibrating resonantly around the room. Poor Christina, she thought. All those visits to the different burger-bars just to please Kit! 'What a woman will do for her favourite man!' she mocked her son smilingly.

'Can I help it if everyone loves me?' He was doing it again, stating the opposite to what he actually believed, but Rebecca could hear the note of warmth in his voice at the gentle praise. Such a sensitive child, she thought achingly, so very much aware of his own vulnerabilities.

'Well, I certainly adore you,' she murmured softly, giving him what she knew he wanted most, which was her loving reassurance. 'I feel as though I'm walking about with my right arm missing without you here.'

'When will you be coming back?' The question was expected but difficult to answer. And her smiling face clouded over again when she remembered her mother lying so very ill in that hospital bed.

'I can't say yet, darling,' she said apologetically. 'Perhaps a couple of days more; hopefully no longer.' Mentally she crossed her fingers, hoping that within a few days she could safely leave her mother to recuperate alone. 'But I'll be sure to let you know when I'm sure.'

'Good, because I want to meet you at the station. Uncle Tom says we can, though Aunt Chrissy will probably be busy working to fill in for you.'

'I know; that's always a problem when one of us goes away,' she acknowledged, sympathising with poor Christina, who would be having to put in the extra hours just to keep up with the orders they were committed to. 'But take care of yourself, darling, and I promise to get back as soon as I can.'

'I wish I was there with you,' he mumbled. 'It only hits me when you're away that I don't know what would happen to me if anything happened to you.'

'Nothing ever will, Kit,' she assured him on a fierce upsurge of maternal protection, another of his insecurities creeping through the light banter he tried so hard to maintain. 'You're my life, you know that. I just wouldn't allow anything to take me away from you.' A sudden blistering vision of his father swam up before her eyes, dark and threatening, pressing down on her, and she shuddered on a fear of black premonition.

They said their goodbyes, and Rebecca replaced the receiver. Her shoulders sagged again, her face along with it, small chin lowering to touch her chest as she took in a couple of careful breaths. It was always hard breaking contact with him, but this time it had been doubly hard because, although she hadn't allowed herself to think about it yet, she knew this visit up here and its ensuing problems was going to force changes into their lives, problems which were bound to cause more problems.

'Husband?' a cool voice enquired behind her.

She turned swiftly, seeing Jay propping up the study door, arms crossed, his expression insolent as he studied her.

'No,' she said, her chin coming up with the kind of challenge she had thrown out for so many years now that she didn't even know she did it any more, clear grey eyes levelling on him, daring him to impose on her privacy further, ask questions he had no right to ask.

He seemed to be considering the idea, the faint cynicism in his expression, making her curl up inside as he ran his eyes over her, trying to delve beneath the layers of protection she wore so thickly around herself. Then he grimaced and pushed himself away from the door.

'If you were reassuring that . . . person on the phone that you'll be home in a few days, then I think it was a little premature of you.'

Rebecca stiffened. 'I have to get back,' she insisted. 'I have commitments of my own. Coming here at such short notice has already placed other people under a strain while they cover for me. I have to get back,' she repeated firmly.

'And your mother?' A dark eyebrow lifted in contempt. 'You just pick her up and put her down again when you're ready to, and damn to the consequences? Don't you think she deserves a little more of your precious time than just a few days' reluctant support?'

'It isn't reluctant,' she stiffly defended. 'It's just . . .' 'Inconvenient' she was going to say, but stopped herself when she realised how that sounded just as bad. 'I have a life of my own now, Jay,' she changed tack coolly, 'responsibilities to meet. I came here as soon as I read your notice—despite those responsibilities—and I would appreciate it if you would afford me the same consideration by accepting that I therefore have to get back to them as soon as I can.'

'And these...responsibilities do not include your mother?' The contempt increased. 'Tell me, Rebecca, because I'm really curious to know...' his eyes slid up and down her erect body before locking with hers '...does whoever he is keep you in the kind of luxury you expected me to pay for? Or is his pocket larger than mine? You certainly dress with designer style,' he derided her. 'So I must hazard a guess that you certainly don't come cheap any more.'

Something violent flashed in her eyes, a brief glimpse of the old impulsive Rebecca, bringing his blue eyes wider in dire challenge of that look, and he watched her hands clench and flex at her sides, the need to reach out and strike him so palpable that it held them both completely still while she fought to quell the urge.

'What I do with my life and with whom I do it is no business of yours,' she told him tightly, finding relief in the angry cut of her tongue. 'Not since the day you left me here alone and didn't give another thought for the naïve young fool you used all summer as an adequate relief for your sexual boredom!'

'Oh, not just adequate, Rebecca,' he drawled. 'You were, as I am sure you must know by now, one hell of a lot more than adequate!'

'God help me, Jay,' she whispered thinly, 'but one more slight on my character, and I shall——'

'What will you do?' he challenged as she stumbled over the fury of words. His hand jerked out to grip her arm, the vicious yank he gave tugging her across the small gap separating them. 'Hit me?' he taunted through cruelly smiling lips. 'Be sure I shall hit you back, Rebecca,' he warned. 'Scream? Who would come running but dear Olivia? And I think she would rather enjoy watching me beat you!'

'I hate you,' she spat, feeling the hot surge of contempt for him flood up inside her. 'I despise what you are and everything you stand for. And if Olivia still possesses that warped kind of view on life then I'm sure you deserve each other! Being married to you must feed it constantly!'

He went still, and Rebecca began to quail inside, fearing that she might have gone too far. Then, 'Married?' he choked. 'Where the hell did you get the idea that Olivia and I are married?'

Rebecca stared at him. 'You mean—you aren't?' The disbelief was clear in her voice, and Jay laughed, a harsh, cutting sound that made her wince.

'I don't need to marry Olivia to get what I want from her,' he bit out scornfully. 'Just as I didn't need to marry you for the same reason!'

His contempt for Olivia and herself made her cringe, and she pulled her arm away from him. 'You are and always were a selfish bastard, Jay,' she said quietly, turning away from him and moving back towards the desk, her slender spine stiff with intention as she picked up the telephone receiver again.

'What are you doing?' he demanded sharply.

'Calling a cab,' she informed him. 'I refuse to stay in this house a moment longer than I have to.'

'You're going damned well nowhere!' he barked, coming to snatch the receiver from her and sending it crashing back on to its rest.

His hands took hold of her again, tugging her around to face him, tall and dark, the power of his attraction hammering down on her senses, their mutual anger, their disdain of the other, their mutual exchange of insults adding an awareness of a different kind, and she shuddered in bitter rejection of it.

'Take your hands off me,' she commanded tightly. 'I can't bear you to touch me!'

'Well, isn't that too bad?' he sneered, pulling her even closer to him so that she felt the burning heat emanating from his angry frame. 'Because it's retribution time, Rebecca, and I am going to take my due!'

His mouth came down hard upon her own, sending her neck snapping back at the force of the kiss, parting her lips and invading her mouth with the sole desire to defile. Yet, as he deepened the kiss with the ruthless lick of his tongue, she felt her own senses stir, instant recognition of a long-lost temptation which set them clambering eagerly to meet it.

When it ended she was white-faced and shaking, her fingers curled around the edge of the desk, nails scoring into the undersurface of the polished wood, breathing completely suspended in an appalled revulsion of both him and herself.

'Rebecca...' Whatever Jay saw as he looked at her, leaning there with the shivers racking her slender frame, eyes wide and staring unblinkingly, it shook him, and it showed in the unsteady way he murmured her name.

She swallowed, willing herself to come out of the dark tumbling black cloud that that kiss had plunged her into. A fine layer of sweat had broken out on her skin, giving her a cold and sickly feeling. Jay couldn't know it, but her sexual urges had been utterly stunted by his ill-use of her ten years ago, and that was the first time a man had kissed her since.

'For God's sake,' he muttered as her grey eyes flickered blankly. 'Don't look at me like that!' He spun away, his dark head bowed, his body tense with anger. 'What did you think I was going to do to you?' he bit out harshly, spinning back to glare at her. 'Rape you?'

The vulgar derision brought her shuddering to her senses, and she straightened, her fingers still tensely curled as she lifted the back of her hand to her bruised mouth. 'I have to leave here,' she said jerkily. 'I can't stay here with——'

'No!' He made as if to grab hold of her again, then dropped his hands with an angry growl as she stiffened into a pillar of stone, staring at him, despising him with her eyes, so repulsed by what had so easily leapt between them that the grey irises had turned opaque. 'No,' he repeated grimly, looking suddenly as pale as she, the smooth skin stretched across his taut lean face. 'Look...' he turned away again, his shoulders hunching inside the expensive cloth of his dark wool jacket '...if it helps any, I apologise for that—loss of control. It won't happen again.' Even though she couldn't see his face, she sensed his grimace of self-derision. 'The reason I came in here,' he went on more calmly, 'was to tell you that Mrs Musgrove has dinner ready. I thought you might like a chance to freshen up before we eat.'

With that he strode to the door, swinging it open and striding through with his broad back erect and his head slightly bent.

Rebecca followed, too drained to do anything else. That kiss had acted like a total ravishing of her soul, ripping open old wounds and laying them bare and bleeding, and her sickened response to it had shaken them both beyond what should have been necessary. She could only be thankful that he didn't seem to know how wildly she had come alive for him then, how that deep dark place in her soul that she had sent all feeling of Jay to had split wide open and let it all flood out again.

He had picked up her case and was moving up the stairs. She went after him, passing his stern ancestors on her way, remembering a time when she used to stand on these stairs as a small child just gazing up at those old faces, wondering if they were devils because they used to look like such grim bad men then to her young impressionable mind.

Perhaps they were, she now found herself concluding. A bad gene passed down through the ages. Then she shivered, thinking of Kit, and thrust the sobering thought away.

In single file they walked along the upper landing, treading paths she had again taken as a child, awed then by the grace and grandeur of the house. Proud, in the naïveté of her youth, that her mother should be the one allowed to care for such a beautiful place, her father allowed to tend the exquisite gardens.

It was years before she began to realise that a pride in Thornley Hall was not hers to have, how that honour belonged to the people who owned it, not the regiment of staff they paid to keep it in its impeccable style.

Funny, that, she found herself thinking as Jay stopped at a door and opened it, walking smoothly inside. But, for all her blind love for the son of this house, she had never once thought of herself as its mistress. Not even during her most imaginative daydreams. She had blindly believed Jay to be hers, but never the rich trappings which automatically came along with him.

'I hope this will suit,' Jay murmured, placing her case on the end of the bed before turning back to face her.

He had withdrawn behind a mask of cool politeness, his feelings under rigid guard. Rebecca stood on the threshold of the room, gazing around without any show of surprise on her studiously blank face. She knew the room, of course. She knew all the rooms in this house, had helped clean them from top to bottom in her time. And this one was known as Cissy's room—not Jay's mother, but his father's sister. Cissy Lorence had been the black sheep of the family, the Lorence who ran away to marry the man she loved, careless of the fact that he was nothing better than a farmer's son. They went off to America and were never heard of again. But this room was still referred to as Cissy's room.

Perhaps it was apt that Jay had allotted it to her, Rebecca mused as she moved further inside, a black sheep herself, in an odd twisted way.

'There's a bathroom through that door,' Jay reminded her, passing her on his way back out of the room. 'If you can be ready in fifteen minutes, then I think Mrs Musgrove will be relieved. Dinner has already been put back an hour; I don't think it will keep much longer.'

The door closed, and she lowered herself on to the bed, still trembling in the aftermath of the ugly scene downstairs, wishing she dared request a tray and just a sandwich to eat up here on her own, but unwilling to reveal the weakness that that request would show. Downstairs Olivia waited to play queen over the dining-room table. And, really, Rebecca did not have the right to deny her her triumph.

'Jay won't marry you, you know!' Olivia's scornful voice twittered down through the years. 'You can tantalise him with that sexy body of yours as often as you like, but, when it comes to it, Jay will marry money, class, good quality stock.'

'Oh—like your father marries his prize bull with only quality breeding-class cows?' she'd drawled back mock interestedly. 'How utterly degrading to the poor woman who gets Jay, then.'

Olivia had not appreciated the clever wit in that reply, but Rebecca had. That younger Rebecca anyway. This older one only saw further proof of just how blind and foolish she had been about Jay.

She forced herself to get up, her movements sluggish as she unlocked her case and selected the least crushed dress she had hurriedly packed that morning.

Was it only that morning when she had read that notice in the paper?

Her head lifted, eyes staring blindly at the plushly quilted lavender-blue satin head-board in front of her. It seemed like a lifetime had gone by.

Ten years at least.

CHAPTER FIVE

REBECCA would have liked to shower the taint of British Rail and hospital from her skin, but there wasn't time. Stripping off her dress, she walked into the bathroom, running water into the creamy marbled porcelain wash-basin, then lifted her gaze to the gold-framed mirror hanging in front of her, seeing the changes the day had already managed to wreak on her smooth-skinned face. Her eyes looked dark, clouded to a turbulent winter grey, her delicate cheekbones promoted by the taut stretching of the tensely held skin covering them. Tiredness was pulling down the soft corners of her mouth—a mouth which still throbbed in the burning memory of Jay's cruel kiss.

She should not be here. Every instinct she possessed was warning her to get away, flee, before her hard-worked-for peace and stability came tumbling down around her.

Lowering her head, she washed her face, using the sweet-scented soap provided to scrub away the day's jaded make-up, swilling her face with fresh cold water which left her feeling a little better if no less depressed.

Taking the pins out of her hair, she brushed it vig-orously, deciding to leave it loose, not used to having it pinned for so long in one stretch. At home she did not need to worry overmuch about her appearance. She dressed casually, in comfortable clothes put together by her own hands, hands which had learned their craft the hard way—by sheer necessity of having to make do and mend.

Meeting Christina had been a big turning-point in her young lonely life. It was she who had suggested she take in sewing from outside—a job women could do from home when they had small children. 'I know some women who would kill to own a suit like that,' Christina had told her, eyeing the little summer cotton outfit Rebecca was wearing with envy. She had made it up out of an offcut of fabric she had bought cheap at the market, running it up on an old treadle machine she'd found languishing in the cellars beneath her small bedsit flat.

From there it went on to renting a more sophisticated industrial machine which would overlock the raw edges and sew the seams in one quick smooth run of the needles, its necessity dictated by the healthy rush of orders she'd had from Christina's showing her suit to the other girls who worked in the huge office block where she was employed as a secretary.

Eventually, her confidence bolstered by the cries of praise for her work which came back to her, she had tried her hand at design, making clothes with better-quality fabrics found by scouring the local market stalls and shops for offcuts and seconds rather than perfect measurements. And within a year she was having to employ another sewer to help her keep up with her orders, a girl she trained herself with patience and understanding, having been through all the trials and tribulations of learning the craft from scratch herself. A natural flair for art made her creations different but easy to wear. Casual yet eye-catching.

Her list of customers grew slowly by word of mouth, branching out like a small spruce until it became a wide and spreading full-grown tree. She found herself with money in the bank, enough to put a mortgage on a small house with a garden for Kit to play in and enough room to convert the ground floor into working units. Christina was so enthusiastic about the whole venture that she had offered to put money into the business for better and more sophisticated machinery. She'd left her job and joined in the fun Rebecca's little empire generated, becoming a fully fledged partner who found it incredible that, with a little time and Rebecca's endless patience, she could soon turn her hand to any of the jobs required in the scheme of things. Outside, in the back garden, Kit played happily with whichever of his friends was due that day while their mothers worked—on a part-time and flexible basis—on his mother's designs.

She had never felt daunted, never worried why or how she had become so successful or whether it was all suddenly going to fail, because the whole thing had grown so naturally, turning at a smooth, manageable pace.

Now she dealt with wholesalers for her fabrics, still haggling for the best bargains, still taking their left-overs from huge bolts of cloth, but getting them cheap enough to keep her prices sensible and her clients coming back year after year, season on season, more like friends than customers. She learned to laugh with them over their fluctuating figures, read at a glance whether they needed an extra inch putting in the waist of a skirt or around the hips without needing to measure or make them aware of the subtle alteration.

On the bed, waiting for her to slip into, lay one of her more exclusive designs, made in a smooth uncrushable silk of a rich jade colour in the dropped-waist twenties style to suit her reed-slender figure. Unembellished. Rebecca preferred simple lines which depended almost entirely on the cut to make the garment. And she smiled a little to herself as she viewed herself in the mirror a few minutes later, remembering how much cutting and re-cutting the prototype to this design had taken before she was satisfied with it, making the first one up, as she usually did, on a piece of badly marred fabric of a similar texture she had picked up cheap for just that purpose; then the poor wretched thing went straight back on to the cutting-table to be carefully unpicked so that she could use it as a template, never finding its way on to anyone's back.

Well, she mused, sliding a last-minute check over herself, it might not quite meet with the elegance of Olivia's lovely dress, but it wasn't bad, not bad at all. Turning towards the door, she lifted her chin and went smoothly out, the softly swirling skirt swishing pleasingly around her knees.

Jay was waiting for her in the hall downstairs, looking magnificent in a formal black dinner-suit which was cut to perfection, the jacket accentuating the breadth of his shoulders, and the trousers outlining the muscled power of his thighs. It was only now as she came towards him, her composure intact, that she began to see the changes in him—the way he wore his clothes, for instance, with an easy sophistication he had not possessed in such great quantity ten years ago. And he was leaner than she remembered, the muscular body more refined. He was a man born to great wealth and power, and that showed too, whereas before Jay had dismissed it, so therefore she had. Now the warning of a ruthless intellect emanated from him, making her shiver slightly because she suspected that he ran his father's companies with the same hard grasp of the reins as Cedric Lorence had.

His piercing gaze was hooded by thick lazy lashes as he watched her come gracefully down the stairs towards him, taking in her loose wavy hair billowing richly around her lightly made-up face, her long legs, slender and perfectly curved, the dress skimming lightly over the feminine shape beneath it.

The blue eyes lifted to hers, and her heart began to thud at the look she glimpsed before he masked it over again. 'You do that to the manner born,' he murmured drily as she reached him.

The remark acted like ice on water, freezing the softened contours of her face, and he grimaced, accepting that he had managed to offend her once again;

whether by intent or accident she wasn't sure, but the way he shoved his hands into the pockets of his black silk trousers hinted at the latter, though she gave no sign of softening as she waited for him to indicate which way they were to go.

'I've just come from ringing the hospital,' he surprised her by saying, 'and your mother is resting peacefully, with no sign of any adverse reaction to your visit.'

'You expected one?' She lifted her fine brows at him, grey eyes as cool and unreadable as a winter sea.

'No,' he said, 'but I thought you might worry about it. Obviously I was wrong.'

He wasn't, and she had been concerned. She had been going to ask him if she could call the hospital to check herself, but she was not going to tell him that, not with that derision glinting in his eyes. As far as she was concerned he could think what he damned well liked.

He took her arm in a polite clasp, and Rebecca quelled the stinging urge to pull away from him, though she walked stiffly at his side as he guided her across the hall and into the drawing-room.

Olivia was sitting on one of the beautifully upholstered settees, her lovely face marred by irritation. 'You're here at last,' she sighed impatiently, her blue eyes narrowing on the way Jay was holding Rebecca. 'I don't know, Jay.' She flicked her angry glance to him. 'It would have been far better if you'd bothered to warn me we would be eating this late. I'm almost faint with hunger!'

'I know, and I apologise,' he said contritely, leading Rebecca further into the room. 'I should have called you and cancelled tonight, but, to be honest, Olivia, I forgot all about you until I saw your car when we arrived.'

'Well, thank you!' she drawled, a soft flush colouring her cheeks, not amused, not amused at all by that small piece of careless honesty from her host. 'If you're both ready, do you think we can eat now?'

'Of course.' Jay dipped his head, his wry look saying he was aware he had offended her also.

It seemed to be his night for offending people, Rebecca mused drily as, keeping a firm grip on her, he changed direction, moving off towards the wide double doors which connected the drawing-room with the elegant dining-room beyond, and Rebecca was woman enough to feel a touch of bitchy satisfaction at seeing Olivia's nose put out of joint as she tagged on sulkily behind them.

A satisfaction which died a quick death once they were seated at the long dining-table and Olivia put herself out to get her own back by monopolising Jay with bright meaningless chatter about all and sundry in the area, deliberately choosing people and subjects Rebecca could know nothing about.

She didn't mind, though, happy to let Olivia shine brightly so long as she kept her sharp barbs from impaling Rebecca instead. She contented herself with picking at the lovely dishes Mrs Musgrove placed in front of her, their aromas all very tempting, but the tension she was living under making it impossible for her to do them any justice.

'More wine, Rebecca?' She started when Jay spoke to her, her eyes flickering upwards to catch the odd intense look in his.

'N-no—thank you,' she refused politely. She had accepted one glass of wine out of good manners, but she was not a drinker of wine, or of any other form of alcohol. The lean life she had led from such an early age had curbed her desire to experiment with alcohol, and now she found she had no palate for it.

The request brought Olivia's attention to her though, and Rebecca waited fatalistically for the subtle crucifixion of her composure to begin.

'Well,' she began lightly enough, 'it's been...nice seeing you again, Becky. Will you be staying long?'

'I shouldn't think so,' she answered vaguely, determined not to give Olivia the satisfaction of knowing anything about her plans if she could help it. 'But no doubt we shall see each other again before I leave.' She smiled a false smile at the other girl and got one back in return.

'Most probably,' Olivia said smoothly, 'since Jay and I spend a lot of time together.' A magnolia-smooth hand reached out to cover Jay's where it lay on the table, staking claim, Rebecca made wry note. 'Perhaps we could even go out one night!' she suggested brightly. 'I could always find someone who would partner you, Becky.'

Yes, but who? Rebecca wondered acidly. The local village tramp? Because that was what her tone implied. 'I haven't come all the way up here to socialise, Olivia,' she informed the other woman coolly. 'My mother is ill; I shall be spending most of my time with her, I should imagine.'

'Then getting back to your own life, no doubt.' Again the derision entered Olivia's tone, setting Rebecca's back up. 'You never were really... close to her, were you?'

'Close enough to now be considering moving back up here if my mother wishes to remain in Thornley,' Rebecca heard herself say impulsively, and was at least satisfied to see two mouths drop in surprise, even if she didn't mean it. There was no way on earth she could move back here. Not with Kit. Not ever with Kit. 'But maybe I can talk her into coming back with me.'

'To where?' Jay put in sharply.

She glanced at him, realising rather smugly that he had no idea where she was living. He hadn't thought to ask before and she wouldn't have told him anyway. So, 'London,' she answered unrevealingly, knowing how big a place it was and how easily one could lose oneself in it.

'Your mother has lived in Yorkshire all her life,' he dismissed that idea with a scathing tone. 'Only an insensitive brute would consider moving her from her roots at this late stage in her life.'

'Then what do you suggest I do?' she challenged him coolly. 'I'm not a fool, Jay; I am able to judge that my mother will not be able to carry on working here when she comes out of hospital. She's already way past the age of retirement as it is, and, as you clearly pointed out earlier,' she added silkily, 'she is my responsibility, not anyone else's.'

'Then, as you suggested just now, you'll have to move back here.' The odd note of triumph in his voice made Rebecca frown. Why should that be an appealing prospect to him?

'My present commitments may make that...difficult,' she prevaricated.

'A man?' Olivia asked juicily.

Rebecca held Jay's gaze for a moment, then turned to look at Olivia. 'Isn't there always?' she drawled, then added smoothly, 'But I also run my own business, and I really can't afford to simply uproot and move it several hundred miles.'

'You—run your own business?' At last she seemed to have impressed Olivia, while Jay's eyes narrowed reassessingly on her.

She didn't look at him. 'Yes,' she confirmed, 'but not the kind that can be moved lock, stock and barrel from one place to another. I design and make ladies' clothes,' she admitted. 'My customers rely on my personal attention. So I have to be where they are, if you get my meaning.'

'Oh,' Olivia pouted, looking disappointed, 'you mean you take in sewing like old Mrs Denver used to do in the village?'

'No,' said Rebecca, rising to her feet, 'I produce under my own label...Salamander,' she added calmly, and enjoyed watching Olivia's mouth drop open again.

'You mean—*you're* Salamander?' Her tone said she didn't believe it.

'Mad, isn't it?' Rebecca agreed, smiling through her smug satisfaction. Salamander was only a small branch of her real work, but comprised the expensive lines for which she made up her designs in only the most exclusive fabrics. It had been Christina's idea to try making up some samples so she could haul them around the best boutiques in London to see what they thought. That was three years ago. Since then the Salamander label had become an envied name in the world of exclusive fashion. Rebecca made only six new outfits each season, and they were snapped up for a small fortune before they'd even got off the drawing-board.

'Is that a Salamander?' Olivia was eyeing her jade silk dress with new eyes now, her expression faintly envious.

'No,' Rebecca smiled. 'This is a—Rebecca. A one-off,' she explained the pun, 'designed and made for my own pleasure.' She flicked her gaze to a still-thoughtful Jay. 'If you don't mind...' she took her chance while she could '...I would like to retire now—it's been a...long day for me.'

'Of course.' He rose smoothly to his feet, his table manners, like most things about him, meticulous.

With their cool goodnights and their rather thoughtful gazes on her, Rebecca made her graceful escape from the room, pausing out in the hall to relax the unbearable tension from her shoulders before straightening again and making for the stairs.

Jay caught her there, coming out of the room and calling her name softly as he closed the door behind him. Rebecca turned, her expression questioning and faintly wary.

'I still have him,' he told her huskily.

She frowned, wondering what he was talking about.

'Salamander,' he enlightened her, and smiled drily as her grey eyes widened on him, the heat running up her cheeks when she realised he had made the connection. 'Why his name of all names for your label, Rebecca?' he asked, moving to stand by the dark polished newel-post to gaze mockingly up at her. 'Could it be that you missed us while you were busy building your little empire?'

She turned away, a cool shutter coming over her delicate features. 'If you mean by that did I miss Salamander?' she answered remotely. 'Then the answer is yes. He was the only true friend I really had in this place. Of course I remember him.'

And, with that, she continued on up the stairs, aware of his narrowed gaze piercing thoughtfully into her back, aware, that in her silly desire to wipe that condescending expression from Olivia's face, she had revealed enough about herself to make him curious to know more.

She shivered, angry with herself for that. She had not come up here to play the prodigal as Jay had oh, so sarcastically mocked at the station. And she certainly had not come here to show them all how very successfully her life had turned out despite their concerted efforts to ruin her! So taking up challenges of any nature was a foolish and dangerous thing to do.

But Salamander was still here? Her weary heart gave a small flutter of pleasure as she moved about her luxurious room, making ready for bed. And she closed her eyes for a moment, allowing herself to wing back through the years to a time when she had used to gallop wild and free on the powerful back of Jay's coveted black stallion, Salamander's long black mane blowing like fine gossamer in the wind while she laughed gaily, taunting the man keeping pace beside her. Jay—her heart creased achingly—Jay grinning at her, urging her on with the challenge in glinting blue gaze, riding Salamander's beautiful sister Salome.

'Why do I always get to ride the stallion while you ride the mare?' she had asked him curiously once, and could still see the wicked glint in his eyes as he'd answered meaningfully,

'I'd much rather be astride a beautiful woman, Becky—I thought you already knew that!'

She moved jerkily, those unwanted waves of nostalgia twisting her insides. She could have sworn on her own life that he loved her then. Sworn it—and probably had, to her own stupid folly.

CHAPTER SIX

REBECCA slept badly, and awoke early, her dreams too disturbing for her to want them to continue once the first lick of daylight began filtering into her room. So she indulged herself in a long soak in a hot bath, hoping it would ease some of the aching tension out of her muscles before the new day's stresses began loading on to her.

Jay had already left for the office when she eventually came downstairs. She knew he had because she had delayed leaving her room until she'd watched the low black sports car sweep smoothly up the drive.

'Good morning, Miss Shaw.' Mrs Musgrove's smile was warm and genuine as Rebecca walked into the large modern kitchen. 'Mr Jay sends his apologies, but he's had to go into the office for a few hours, and said to tell you that when you're ready to get Jimmy to drive you into Harrogate.'

'Jimmy still works here?' Her eyes brightened, a new warmth entering the deep grey depths. Jimmy Tiler was the man who had taken her father's place after his death, tending to the gardens and playing chauffeur when it was required of him.

'Yes.' Mrs Musgrove smiled. 'I think he means to go on forever, does Jimmy,' she murmured drily. 'Like your mother, from what I hear.' Then, because a sudden stiffness entered the atmosphere, she said carefully, 'I have never met her, Miss Shaw; Mr Jay had to employ me to cover for her when she took ill, but I know she's thought well of here at the Hall, and I would like to assure you that I am not hankering after stealing her position here. I'm temporary, that's all, until your mother gets back on her feet.'

Rebecca smiled to show she had not been wondering about Mrs Musgrove's position there. But the smile soon died when she recalled the conversation she'd had at the dinner table the night before. She had not been speaking off the top of her head when she had told Jay that her mother was never going to be able to work here again. It had taken only one look at her mother in that hospital bed to know that her working days were over.

She ate a light breakfast of coffee and toast, then went to ring Kit, taking strength from his light warm chatter. Then she spoke to Christina, checking on the business, and on Kit himself, and reassuring herself that everything was running smoothly in her absence.

'How was it?' Christina asked once the main business was out of the way.

'Difficult,' she admitted honestly. 'It's weird, but I can't seem to sort out how I feel about anything up here any more,' she said with a frown. 'It was awful seeing my mother lying there so frail and ill like that. I suppose we all think of mothers as immortal, made to go on forever... I'm going to have problems when she recovers properly, Chrissy,' she murmured worriedly. 'She's going to need looking after, and I'm not sure yet just how I'm going to be able to manage it, taking into account all the underlying problems which will inevitably come with her.'

'And Jason Lorence?' Christina put in carefully. 'Have you seen him yet?'

'Oh, yes.' Rebecca's mouth twisted. 'I'm standing in his study right now,' she drawled, 'playing reluctant guest to his reluctant host.'

'My God,' Chrissy gasped, 'how did that happen?'

'A long story,' Rebecca sighed, 'and one which will have to wait until I get back.'

'Well, don't worry about Kit—he's fine with us, you know that.' Christina took the hint easily enough; she had known Rebecca long enough now to know not to delve where Rebecca did not wish it.

Jimmy was pleased to see Rebecca, and they chatted lightly about all kinds of things as he drove her to the hospital. He talked about Thornley, and her mother, and the few changes which had been made about the estate without touching on any sensitive subjects.

Never a nosy man, and always one who saw more than his quiet manner gave him credit for, Jimmy, perhaps more than anyone else here ten summers ago, knew just how close she and Jay had been.

She spent the day with her mother, relieved to find her looking less frail when she entered the unit that morning. And slowly, with a great deal of wariness on both sides, they began to build tentative grounds for a new relationship. Rebecca made no mention of Kit, and her mother did not question the results of that ultimatum both she and Jay's father had set Rebecca ten years before. For Rebecca's part she was still too uncertain how she was going to tackle the problem of Kit and his Yorkshire ties. Telling her mother about him was, she accepted at least, a *fait accompli* situation, but she couldn't face it yet, not until she'd had time to consider very carefully what she was going to do. Because there was one thing she was positive about: Jay was not going to find out. She could not afford to let him.

She was reading quietly to her mother when Jay appeared later that afternoon. She hadn't heard him arrive, the sound-muffling floor surface allowing him to come upon them silently. And it was her mother who saw him first, a lopsided smile lighting her sleepy face as she murmured, 'Jay! How nice to see you!'

'Well, you're looking better today, Lina,' he said, coming to bend over the bed to place a fond kiss on her worn old cheek, looking lean and alive, bringing into the room with him a kind of vital force which set the hairs on the back of Rebecca's neck tingling. 'I wonder just what has brought on this transformation?' he teased.

Tears entered her mother's eyes. 'Oh, Jay...' the old lady whispered shakily. 'Thank you for finding her...' Her thin hand slid across the bed-covers to find Rebecca's and clasp on to it tightly. 'You don't know how much it means to me to have Rebecca back at last.'

'I think I do, Lina,' he said quietly, his eyes straying across the bed to clash darkly with Rebecca's.

'It was all my fault, you know,' her mother went on weepily. 'I sent her away—such a wilful child, such a difficult child to control. But I had no right to forsake her as I did!' she added thickly, turning her tearful gaze on Rebecca. 'I didn't, Becky, and I've spent all these years regretting it.'

'Don't upset yourself, Mummy!' Moved by the depth of guilt she could hear in her mother's voice, but also afraid that in her distress she might say something she shouldn't, Rebecca stood up, laying the book aside to smile fondly at her. 'It doesn't matter any more. The past is the past, and best forgotten now, don't you think?'

'Oh, yes,' her mother sighed, 'I would much prefer to forget it if I only could.'

Sleep took her quickly, as if the short burst of emotion was all it took to exhaust her, and both Jay and Rebecca stood watching her for some minutes before he lifted his head and looked at Rebecca.

'Did she send you away?'

She hesitated over her reply, her own gaze hooded by the long sweep of her lashes, then said, 'Yes,' aware that there were enough deceptions littering the situation without adding to them unnecessarily.

'Why?' he wanted to know, those eyes still fixed on her averted profile. 'Did she find out about us, Becky? Is that it?'

Just to hear him call her Becky for the first time was enough to send a tingling shiver through her, and she bit down hard on her bottom lip, wondering why he sounded so stunned by the idea, when he had to remember how casually he too had cast her out.

'As I just said to my mother——' her chin came up, her eyes as cool and unimpassioned as a bottomless lake '—the past is the past, and best left to lie.'

He held that look for a while, cogs busily turning in that sharp, shrewd brain. He knew there were secrets here, things that he did not know about. But not many, the way Rebecca remembered it. If Jay had decided to thrust all the nasty memories away then she supposed that was his prerogative, but if he could be that heartless there was no use in going back over it all, and she hardened her own heart against him, turning away from that piercing blue stare to gather together her things in readiness to leave.

He watched her in silence, every move and graceful gesture warning him that she had withdrawn behind the thick shield he had already become familiar with. The old Rebecca had worn her emotions on her face, and given free rein to them whenever they surfaced, whether it was anger, delight, or hot searing passion. But this new Rebecca revealed hardly anything at all, her composure almost unbreakable.

Except when he'd kissed her. And then the emotion had broken through the restraints, shocking him by the depth of their revulsion, leaving him feeling sick with shame and angry that he had allowed his own emotions to better him with such devastating violence.

They drove most of the way back to Thornley in silence, neither seeming to want to make light conversation. Rebecca had a lot to think about, not least her concern over her mother. She'd had a chance today, while her mother had been resting, to speak to the doctor. Although her mother was making reasonable progress, he had told Rebecca that she would never be very steady on her feet again. 'And the pneumonia has weakened her chest,' he said. 'In short, Miss Shaw, your mother's health has been damaged pretty badly by the unfortunate chain of events. She is going to need careful watching. No more work. No more living alone.'

'I'm afraid I shan't be in for dinner tonight,' Jay said suddenly, making her jump because the silence between them had gone on for so long. 'A business dinner I can't pull out of.' He turned to glance at her, grimacing.

'That's quite all right,' she answered coolly. 'I'm not staying with you as a true guest, so don't feel you have to entertain me.'

'Maybe I would rather be entertaining you,' he murmured, throwing her another glance.

She looked away, her profile a series of gentle contours, perfectly composed. But the dull throb his husky remark set up inside her was by no means composed. She had picked up on the underlying meaning, and wanted to reject it out of hand. Only she couldn't, because Jay was beginning to affect her in the way he'd always used to do, right where it hurt her the most in the badly scarred tissue around her heart.

The rounded slopes of her breasts moved up and down on a heavy sigh. She wished she wasn't here with him. She wished the whole risky situation had never arisen.

'If you and your mother can make your peace, Rebecca,' he said quietly, 'then don't you think we could try to do the same?'

No, she thought bleakly. We could never do the same. Turning again, she looked levelly at him, seeing the Jason Lorence he was now. A well-cared-for, sleekly honed and extremely attractive man. A man who wore his maturity of body and mind as easily as he wore the mantle of power he had inherited from his father.

The other, younger Jay had been excitingly reckless, ready to encourage her into any mad prank she might have come up with, seeming to love her wildly impulsive nature, her sheer zest for living life to the full.

She had known the exciting power of his sexuality, felt her own leap deliriously up to meet it in that sensual battle of woman against man; seen that hard-muscled body of his stripped and naked, gleaming beneath the silvered sheen of a full moon, stirring her to the heights of a passion she had thought impossible to reach by just simply standing there, looking, their eyes making love without needing to touch.

Her senses were heightened, pleading for some kind of acknowledgement that they were there, for a freedom to express themselves in a way they had not been allowed to do for ten long barren years. But she kept them contained. Just as they had moulded her into the woman she was now, the ensuing years had moulded the playful and passionate youth into a calm and collected man. And he was all the more dangerous for it, because he seemed able to make her aware of him, if only by this dangerous way she had adopted of comparing him with the old Jay she once knew.

'I don't think so, Jay,' she therefore answered flatly. 'Unlike my mother and I, we no longer have anything to offer each other.'

'You really believe that?' His hands clenched momentarily on the steering-wheel. 'I don't,' he muttered gruffly. 'I damned well don't!'

Her eyes flickered on to him, startled by the roughened texture in his voice. He flashed her a look, a single tenth of a second of his stinging gaze scraping down her slender figure, and it took only that for her to know just exactly what he meant.

She'd seen that look before—many times. He still desired her! Hotly and as passionately as he had done ten years ago! Fiercely, with no thought for consequences or convention or what that desire could do to them!

In confusion she turned away, her lips tightening with a fear and distaste. 'Forget it, Jay!' she told him in a deadly voice. 'I'm no longer that foolishly impressionable and stupidly gullible girl I was ten years ago—I grew up!' she informed him bitterly. 'Quickly and thoroughly, on lessons ruthlessly taught by you!'

The car came to a jerking stop outside the house, and Rebecca climbed out, limbs trembling with an anger and contempt and enough desperation to send her walking quickly into the house. He caught her up in the hall, swinging her around to face him. Angry; as angry and disturbed as she.

'I'm getting just a bit fed up of these loaded remarks you keep throwing at me!' he ground out harshly. 'You left me ten years ago, Rebecca, and I think it's damned time you too recognised that point!'

She stared at him, utterly stunned by the depths to which he had managed to bury the truth. 'Think what the hell you like!' she told him, so angry that the air was being sucked in and out of her lungs in short sharp gasps. 'But let go of me! I'm not a rag doll for you to tug around whenever you feel like it!'

'No,' he snapped. 'You're a hard and embittered woman, who, for some twisted reason known only to yourself, has decided that whatever happened here ten years ago was everyone's fault but your own!'

'That's right,' she agreed, tugging uselessly at her arm. 'Hard, embittered, and not available—for you or any other man to use again!'

'And Kit?' he inserted tightly. 'Where does that leave your "darling Kit"?' he jeered.

Her grey eyes flashed, the storm turning to an icy blizzard in her eyes. 'It leaves Kit where he has always been,' she answered him coldly. 'The exception to an otherwise unbroken rule. He owns me, heart, body and soul! And not you, nor your...old attractions——' she said that derisively '—will ever, *ever* ruin that!'

She tugged, and he let her go so that she could spin away from him, shaking so badly that she could barely place one foot in front of the other as she moved towards the stairs.

'Yet, like me, he hasn't needed to marry you to make you his willing slave...' Jay sneered behind her, and the depth of his derision swirled over her in hard cruel waves. 'And—like me again, I suppose—he's probably found he can take what he wants from you without having to bother with such silly conventional things as marriage!'

'That's right,' she agreed, giving him nothing— nothing, yet telling him everything if he was perceptive enough to hear it. 'Like you in many ways—except the one most important one.' She turned slowly back to look at him, eyes as disdainful as his tone had been. 'You see, Kit loves me. I am the only person in his world who really matters. And neither he nor I need proof, written, vowed or otherwise, to know, unequivocally, that that is true.'

Something moved inside him, and she held the look with a hard contemptuous one of her own for a moment before turning back to the stairs, her composure locked firmly in place.

'And does this—wonderful paragon of a man know about your abortion?'

Rebecca went still, her body jerking as though Jay had just plunged a knife cleanly into her back.

'Or have you preferred to keep that particularly juicy feature of your life from him? Not many men can condone the destruction of an unborn child, Rebecca. It somehow doesn't fit in with the rosy view they prefer to hold of their women, does it?'

'You should know, Jay.' She forced herself to move again, refusing to look back at him a second time in case her control snapped and she flew at him with her nails. 'You're supposed to be a man, after all.'

As an exit line it was perfect, and Rebecca had enough left in her to feel a sharp sense of satisfaction that she had managed to silence him. And she went on up the stairs, her spine straight, her chin held high. It was only once she was safely hidden behind the closed door of her room that she wilted, sinking in shivering reaction on to the bed.

'The cruel bastard,' she whispered, rocking herself as if in the throes of some deep and clenching pain, 'the cruel, unfeeling bastard!'

There was snow that night, falling from the sky in silent glory, covering the countryside in a blanket of glistening white. When she rang Kit the next morning he was beside himself to know if she was snowed in. 'They said on the news that Yorkshire is virtually cut off!' he informed her. 'Snow-drifts as high as a house!'

'Now there's an exaggeration if I ever heard one,' Rebecca derided. 'Yes, it's snowed, and yes, it's thick on the ground. But the roads are passable and as usual the media are out to cause panic.' But she bit her bottom lip, wondering if there was any truth in Kit's claim. The idea of being snowed in here did not appeal at all. She had already made up her mind the night before that she would be going back to London tomorrow. Even if it did mean leaving her mother a day or two sooner than she wished to.

She couldn't stay here any longer. It was beginning to hurt too much.

Her mother was tired and tetchy that day when she visited, seeming to be worrying over something which made her restless and anxious. Rebecca tried soothing her by reading to her again, but it didn't seem to help, and she was aware that the nurse on duty popped in to check on her more often than she had done the day before, her brief uninformative smile telling Rebecca nothing.

By lunchtime the skies had darkened, the clouds heavily laden with a fresh load of snow. And the urgency to get back to London before she was really trapped up here had her leaning over her mother to try to explain to her why she had to go.

'No!' Lina Shaw cried, reaching out to grip tightly on to Rebecca's hand. 'Don't leave me, Becky—not again...please don't leave me!'

'Please, Mummy,' she pleaded thickly, hating herself for having to do this. 'I promise I'll come back to see you next weekend...' Even if it meant using a damned snow-plough to get here! she told herself guiltily. She was willing to do the same every weekend until her mother was well enough to leave the hospital, if necessary, but she could no longer stay in such close proximity to Jay! 'Please try to understand that I have commitments I have to see to. Things I can't leave for other people to do for me!' She had already told her mother about her business, and how time-consuming it was.

'I don't want you to go, Becky...' The tears began filling the distressed eyes again, and, feeling utterly wretched with herself, Rebecca sat down on the edge of the bed to gently pull her mother into her arms.

'I love you, Mummy,' she whispered, saying it for the first time, and finding, to her own surprise, that she actually meant it. 'I don't want to leave you here. But Jay will visit you, you know that. And I'll come back at the weekend...'

'No, you won't,' the frail old woman whispered wretchedly. 'You'll go away again and forget all about me!' She began to cry with weak shallow pathetic little sobs which wrung at Rebecca's heart and made her hold her closer.

'Don't do this, Mummy,' she pleaded thickly. 'Please don't cry—I can't bear it!'

'I know you must hate me,' the strained voice groaned through the sobs. 'Oh, but you have to forgive me, Becky! You have to! I can't go on living with it otherwise! I j-just can't!'

'I forgive you,' her daughter stated fiercely. 'Of course I forgive you!'

'All these years,' she sobbed on, her gnarled fingers worrying in Rebecca's hair, clutching, holding on tightly as if she was terrified of letting go. 'It's been eating away at me, Becky, eating and eating until I couldn't take it any more!'

'Ssh,' Rebecca soothed, moved by the depth of guilt and pain her mother was suffering. 'Ssh, it doesn't matter any more. None of it matters except your getting yourself well again.'

'Oh, but it does matter!' she quavered bleakly. 'We all let you down so badly! Me, Mr Lorence, Jay...' The twisted side of her mother's face looked grotesque in its wretched torment. 'Such a terrible crime we committed against you, Becky, such an unforgivable crime! A baby, God help us all, plotting to destroy a poor defenceless baby! My God!' she choked, the plaintive cry wrenching her thin frail body. 'Jay's child—my own grandchild—forfeited for the sake of foolish pride! No excuse on this earth can make that right! Nothing... I——'

Something tormented wrenched inside her mother. Rebecca felt it happen with a terrible surge of fear, her eyes stark and panicked as she laid the suddenly limp body back against the pillows. 'Mummy!' she cried out shrilly. 'For God's sake—I didn't do it! You have a grandson, darling—a wonderful, healthy nine-year-old grandson!'

Then all hell broke loose around her, beginning with the monitor beside the bed letting out a high-pitched warning sound. And she turned wildly, searching with fear-glazed eyes for the nurse, then froze, completely and totally, as her gaze skidded to rest on the tall dark figure standing at the bottom of the bed. He looked shattered, his eyes turned silver with shock, skin white and drawn, ageing him ten years in just a few short but devastating seconds.

People came running from everywhere, jostling against him in their urgency to reach Lina Shaw, reaching out and bodily lifting Rebecca from the bed, pushing her aside so they could go down in an urgent rugby scrum and begin battle with the emergency they were so specifically trained for. Yet none of it broke the numbing eye-to-eye contact between Rebecca and Jay.

He overheard, and now he knows, was all she could think. Once again he had come upon them silently, and overheard every damning, mind-blowing and unequivocal word.

Then someone was taking Rebecca by the shoulders, murmuring something soothing to her, and carefully leading her out of the room. Her lashes flickered, the grey eyes lowering away from Jay's, and she allowed herself to be pushed gently into a chair, then left, with a mumbled apology, to shiver in a deep and violent shock on her own.

When he joined her she had no idea, only that suddenly he was sitting beside her, his hand reaching out to gather her twisted ones in his. They didn't speak, and she did not try to push him away, her mind and body set in a stiff waiting pose until eventually, aeons later, a white-coated doctor appeared in front of them and said very quietly, 'It's all right, Miss Shaw. Your mother is all right. Just a slight seizure, brought on by overexcitement, but nothing to worry about. We've sedated her now, and we'll probably keep her like that for a couple of days, just to be on the safe side.'

Rebecca looked up, nothing going on behind her blank staring gaze. She glanced at the doctor's quietly sympathetic face, then at the room beyond him where the monitor bleeps were once again reassuringly steady. Then back down to where her hands lay cocooned in Jay's, his wrist lean and hairy, the pristine cuff of his shirt showing bright white against the dark grey stuff of his jacket sleeve.

And suddenly, with a blinding flash of insight which threw her into total shock, she realised what she had never realised before, not ten years ago, not two days ago when she made her long and reluctant journey up here, and not even today when she listened to her mother's guilt come spewing wrenchingly out.

That it didn't matter. None of it mattered. Not the way her mother had turned her back on her when she needed her the most. Not Jay and his cruel rejection. Not even his father with his callous ultimatum and nasty pay-off—or even her own bitter sense of betrayal. That, in the last analysis, the only thing which really mattered was that she had not done what everyone believed her to have done. That ten years of hating, of pretending she no longer existed, ten years of what she now knew to be a guilt her mother had carried around with her, were all for nothing. Because Kit was alive and well and happy. A child rejected in the womb by all those who feared his power over them was alive, and if she had not gone away, if she had stuck to her principles and faced them all with the reality of it, then those ten long gruelling years could have been clean ones, where honesty and justice would have won over bitterness, guilt and disgrace.

CHAPTER SEVEN

REBECCA'S face lifted, her eyes searching for and finding Jay's, fixed darkly on her. And her chin came up, warning of that pride she had fought hard and long to earn, challenging him to dare say she had no right to it.

'Is he my son, Rebecca?' he asked her grimly.

She didn't reply; couldn't. The truth stuck thickly in her throat, and she got up, moving jerkily to go and stand in the opening to her mother's room, her arms folded tightly across her breasts as she stood there, viewing that poor guilt-ridden figure sleeping on the bed.

This was all her own fault! she reproached herself. She should never had gone away from here ten years ago! She should never have let those blasted Lorences intimidate both her and her mother! And she should never have even considered leaving her mother's bedside so soon when she knew deep down in her heart that the poor dear was not ready for another parting!

Tears split her vision, the guilt coming to rest weightily upon her own shoulders. Kit would have been safe enough with Christina and Tom! She'd really had no dire need to go rushing back to London just yet!

It was Jay who had been driving her away again, she accepted bitterly. Jay, and the force of his attraction. And herself, and the fear of her own.

'Look...' he came up behind her, not touching her but close enough for her to pick up on the determined way he was holding on to his self-control '...we can't do any more for her here today,' he said. 'And the sky was black with snow when I came in here. Let's get home before we're snowed in here...'

Home . . . The word did nothing nice to her. Home for her was several hundred miles away, in a neat little house which was a busy cottage industry and home rolled into one.

Moving into the room, she collected her belongings still lying across the spare chair by her mother's bed. She paused when she'd picked them up, turning to level one last guilty glance on her mother, then bent to place a tender kiss on her hollowed cheek. 'I love you, Mummy,' she said grimly, then straightened, her face settling into a cool mask as she walked past Jay and towards the lifts.

Jay was right about the snow. It was already tumbling thickly from the sky. And in a way she was relieved, because it meant he had to use his full concentration on getting them back on the dark slippery roads, rather than beginning his interrogation of her.

Once inside, Rebecca made for the stairs, hoping to escape to her room before Jay entered the house. But the chance had been slim at most, and his, 'Not so fast,' coming with grim intent from just behind her had her sighing defeatedly as she turned to look at him. 'The study,' he said, and, without a word, she went, preceding him inside, and taking off her coat before going to sit down in one of the winged chairs to lean forward and warm her cold hands on the roaring log fire in the grate.

Jay followed, his mood grim as he too removed his big overcoat and discarded it before taking the chair opposite her.

'Is he my son?' He repeated the question she had left hanging in the air back at the hospital.

She laughed, a hard sound that came nowhere near humour. 'According to most people, no,' she said, remembering the terrible accusations, the debasing challenges on her ability to know whose baby she was carrying; the anger, the hostility, the utter, dizzying bewilderment as to what was happening to her; the pain of rejection and the cold numbing fear of what she was going to do, where she was going to go, and how she was going to manage at the vulnerable age of sixteen with a baby and nobody to care whether they lived or died.

'That isn't what I asked,' he snapped, anger slicing silver into the blue eyes. 'I asked you if you and I have a son I know nothing about!'

Again she laughed, and again it jarred. 'No, you don't have a son you know nothing about,' she answered sarcastically, thrusting her chin out to challenge him word for prevaricating word. 'Though you may have a son you once knew about who was—to your reckoning—got rid of in the name of family pride!' she allowed.

'What are you talking about?' He actually managed to look utterly blank. 'I never have and never would condone any woman taking away her child's right to survival—no matter what the damned circumstances may be!'

'No?' She got up, hating him, despising him as she despised his ability to lie—even to himself, judging by his look of angry bewilderment. 'So the big fat cheque I was given on your behalf to abort my child had nothing to do with you, did it?'

Jay shot to his feet, his face draining into a mask of angry affront. 'Now, just wait a minute...' He stopped her turning her back by grabbing her arm and holding her still in front of him. 'I never wrote you a cheque,' he gratingly denied, 'authorised or otherwise! So stop trying to make me out a callous murderer of defenceless babies!'

'Why,' she sneered, 'when that is exactly what you are?'

'Now just listen here, Rebecca...' And if she thought she was full of burning aggression then Jay's mood eclipsed her, his fingers biting into the tender flesh of her arm. 'I won't allow you to speak to me like that! Hell! I worshipped the blasted ground you walked on!' he bit out huskily.

'You know I worship the ground you walk on, Becky!' She had believed that passionate cry once. She would not do so again.

'I refuse to discuss it!' she told him, wrenching herself away from him to turn back to the fire, shaking so badly that she had to wrap her arms around her body to try to control herself.

He seemed to need a moment to get a control on himself, and she could hear him breathing harshly behind her, then he bit out in a low, driven voice, 'Is the son you have tucked away somewhere in this God-forsaken country mine or not?'

Not! she wanted to yell at the top of her voice. *Not now, not ever!*

She continued to stare at the fire, her eyes as hot and angry as the blazing logs alight in the grate. And inside her ten years of bitter disillusionment came rumbling up to the surface of her being, holding her stiff and trembling like a volcano on the very edge of eruption, making her want to scream, kick, maim him as he had once mortally maimed her! Wanting to lie to him, feel the sheer joy of denying him the right to call Kit his son! Then, just as bitterly, she thought, why should she? Why *should* she lie about Kit's conception? He was *her* son, and she was proud to be his mother—no matter how his father felt about his part in it all!

Spinning around, eyes alight with that burning pit of hatred, she said through clenched white teeth, 'Yes, he's your son—for all the difference it has ever made to him, thank God!'

His reaction surprised her; rather than his calling her a liar, or demanding she justify that statement by offering him unassailable proof, rather than his questioning her ability to even know who Kit's father was, she watched instead all the colour drain from his face, as a sneer the likes of which she had never seen on a human face before work at his drawn features.

'I could strangle you for this, Rebecca...' he whispered hoarsely. 'I could put my hands around your lovely slender neck and throttle the bloody life out of you! How dare you keep my own flesh and blood hidden away from me for ten damned years?'

Alarmed by the surge of violence pulsing in him, she stepped jerkily back, her heel coming up hard against the brass fender and almost overbalancing her. Jay's hands flew out, grabbing her shoulders to pull her upright, then held on, closing in to crush the slender bones.

'Afraid, are you?' he taunted, his eyes nothing more than two fine slits of silver threat. 'You should be, my little torment. My God, you should be!'

Hostile defiance shone bright in her gaze as she held challengingly on to his, the bitterness always running close to the surface of her grievances against this man, pulsing between them, holding them both rigid as animosities culminating over ten long years sparked from one to the other then back again.

'He's my son, Jay,' she claimed, her possessiveness so clear that it made him shudder. 'Mine! Do you hear? The only part you had in the making of him was a brief ejaculation of sheer animal enjoyment!'

His palm, making sharp contact with her cheek, brought her swaying to a gasping stop. 'Don't you ever degrade his existence like that again!' he bit out harshly, eyes spitting contempt at her.

Her cheek stung, the corner of her lips throbbing where his thumb had caught it. Jay pushed himself away from her, turning his back while he tried with difficulty to harness some control over his own raging temper as the justifiable blow brought her sinking down through her own pain and anger to a calmer level of sanity.

'I'm—sorry,' she whispered in pained remorse. He was right on that if nothing else. She should not degrade Kit's being like that.

He turned to shrivel her with a look, his head jerking on that strong-muscled neck. Then he was looking away again, down at his feet, his hands thrusting into his trouser pockets, and the silence throbbed between them, cluttered with a tempest of emotion too complicated to draw any sense from.

'Ring him,' he said suddenly, spinning on her again, full-bodied this time and threatening.

Rebecca's eyes widened blankly on him. 'What?' she said in bewilderment.

'Call him up,' he clipped, reaching out to grab her arm and drag her towards the desk. He picked up the receiver and thrust it at her. 'Ring *our* son!' he barked at her. 'I presume you do have a way of getting in touch with him? So——' The phone was thrust at her once again '—do it now! I want to hear his voice!'

Trembling with reaction, fearfully aware that Jay was holding on to control by a mere thread and quite likely to hit her again if she wasn't careful, she dropped her eyes to the telephone and, with a fumbling index finger, managed to dial the set of numbers which would connect her with Christina's house.

Her throat was dry and blocked by a bank of thickening tears. The ringing tone stopped, and Christina's voice came clear and bright down the line to her.

'Hi, Chrissy,' she greeted her rustily, and had to cough to clear her throat, her eyes flickering up to Jay's face then nervously away again. 'H-how's Kit?'

'Teasing the life out of poor Tom,' she was told, Christina obviously not hearing the strained emotion throbbing in Rebecca's voice. 'They went ice-skating today, as per agenda. And poor Tom went a cropper on his backside and had to be helped off the ice by a hysterical Kit!'

'Put him on, will you?' She couldn't even find a dutiful laugh, and it was then that her friend recognised the tension.

'Something wrong, Becky?' she asked sharply.

'No!' she assured her, her grey eyes opening wide in an effort to hold back the tears. 'Everything's fine!' If you don't count total disaster! 'Just put Kit on, will you? I—I need to speak to him.'

'Sure...' Chrissy drawled, not believing her for a second. But she went off to find Kit, and Rebecca could hear her calling out to him while Jay's eyes lanced her with more contempt.

'So, Kit's the ever-faithful lover, is he?' he mocked tightly. 'You bitch! You've been talking to my son twice a day on my telephone! You bitch!' he repeated thickly.

'Hi, Mum!' Rebecca blinked at the sound of that bright familiar voice, and the tension growing inside her began to buzz in her head. 'Did Aunt Chrissy tell you about Uncle Tom?' He set off laughing, with no idea that his mother was almost dying of grief on the other end of the line. 'I tell you, it was the funniest thing I've ever seen in my life! Off he went, as confident as can be, saying, "Stay there, Kit, old boy, while I..."'

She heard no more. The phone was rudely snatched from her hand, and she had to stand there, watching Jay's face as he listened to his son's voice for the first time, his colour greying by the second, the emotion he was experiencing drawing the lines of his face into a taut downward curve.

Then she saw it, and her pumping heart stopped dead, as Jay lifted his accusing gaze back to her: his eyes were swimming with tears, his tightly held mouth working on a crush of emotion which was totally breaking up his composure.

He thrust the receiver back at her, and she watched him anxiously as he turned away, moving like a drunkard to go and throw himself down in the chair, burying his dark head in his hands.

'Anyway,' Kit was trilling on innocently, 'it took a bit of coaxing, but I got him back on the ice again, and he managed to stay upright this time! Next time we go I've promised to take him a cushion to put down his trousers—— Hey!' His laughing protest rang shrilly in her head, a part of her mind registering that Tom must have come up and cuffed him one for his cheek, while the other part of her was anxiously fixed on Jay. 'When are you coming home, Mum?'

Rebecca jumped, startled by the question, and too numb to think of a sensible reply. She spun her back on Jay's hunched frame and struggled to pull herself together. Jay moved behind her, and she stiffened, expecting him to come back and grab the phone from her, tell Kit who he was and what a deceitful bitch his mother was! Fear leapt out in all directions, stinging along her spine to send it so erect it felt as if it were in spasm. Then she heard the chinking sound of glass on glass, and realised with a dizzying wave of relief that Jay was pouring himself a stiff drink.

'Listen to me, Kit...' she managed to gather some semblance of order from the ragged mess of her foggy brain '...I-I'm afraid I've been snowed in here, and I really can't say when I'm going to be able to——'

'I told you so!' he chanted smugly. 'Didn't I tell you so?'

'Yes.' She smiled despite the tension in her face muscles. 'Yes, you certainly told me so.' And, for some reason, hot tears filled her aching throat. 'I miss you, darling...' she murmured thickly. 'I'm sorry about the delay.'

'It's OK,' he dismissed, but Rebecca could hear the disappointment in his voice. 'I suppose I shall have to put up with Aunt Chrissy and Uncle Tom for a little while longer,' he sighed, teasing the two people who were obviously listening at the other end of the line.

When she turned back to the room, her goodbyes safely got through, Jay was back in the chair, sitting hunched over the half-full whisky glass.

She chewed uncertainly on her bottom lip for a while, not sure what she should do next, then took in a deep breath and walked over to take the other chair, knowing that this was really only the beginning.

'Tell me his name—his full name,' he demanded, not lifting his head from the grim contemplation of his glass.

'Kit—Christopher Jason Shaw,' she told him quietly.

His grimace was accompanied by a shake of his dark head. 'Well, I suppose that's something at least. His birthday?' he demanded next.

'M-march,' she stammered. 'He will be ten years old on the twentieth of March.'

He nodded, taking the information in. The glass lifted to his lips, and he gulped at it, swallowing tensely. A silence fell between them then, while Rebecca watched and waited, having enough sensitivity to see that Jay was still labouring under the severest kind of shock.

'Who does he look like?'

Tears washed her eyes, the whole thing becoming too much to bear in one mad blow. 'You,' she whispered. 'He looks like you.' And she dropped her head into her hands, fighting to stop the past from closing so painfully in on her.

'God in heaven,' she heard him whisper hoarsely, 'what the hell did I do to you ten years ago to make you want to keep our son from me?'

Her head came up, her eyes darkened with pained derision. 'But I wrote to you, Jay!' she reminded him wretchedly. 'You keep looking at me as though I've committed some terrible crime against you—but I wrote to you telling you I was pregnant! You have to remember it!' and suddenly it was Rebecca full of bitterness and Jay under attack. 'I begged you to come home and help me! But you didn't even bother to reply!'

'A letter?' His head shot up, genuine bewilderment on his grim hard face. 'I received no letter from you!' he denied.

'Oh—do stop claiming your own innocence!' she flared, sick of it, sick of the whole nasty business. 'Of course you received it! Your——'

'Are you sure you ever posted it?' he mocked cynically.

'Yes, of course I'm sure.' She remembered the day quite clearly. It had been throwing down with rain, and she had just received a positive answer to her pregnancy test. She had written to him on one of those special blue airmail letters, begging him to come home, telling him how frightened she was, how she did not know what to do! Then she'd run out into the pouring rain to post it, her thin anorak pulled closely around her as she'd run along the lane to the corner where the post-box was. Then Olivia had driven up beside her. 'For God's sake, Becky—what are you doing out in this weather?' Her usual scornful tone had passed right over her head, she had been so preoccupied.

'I have to post a letter,' she had told her, not even stopping walking.

The little black Mini Olivia drove had then kept pace beside her, the window wound down so that Olivia could mock her with her eyes. 'That's stupid,' she had said, and put her hand out of the window. 'Give the letter to me; I'll post it for you. You'll be drowned if you stay out in this much longer.'

Not sure she wanted to hand such a vital letter over to anyone else but the post-box, Rebecca had hovered for a moment, but the rain was heavy, and she was beside herself with worry, and already the sickness which went with her condition had been grabbing at her stomach all day. So she had handed over the letter, and Olivia had smiled condescendingly and driven off, promising to post it for her. She'd even stayed where she was, raindrops dripping off her hair on to her nose as she'd watched the little black Mini reach the bend in the road and stop, and Olivia's wave as she'd jumped out of the car and put the letter into the box.

Of course the letter was posted! she recalled on a fresh surge of contempt for him. His own father had confirmed it when he had had her ordered up to the big house and begun ranting and raving at her just a week later, telling her that his son denounced any responsibility for her condition, and if she was intending trying to blackmail Jay into marrying her then she had another think coming—because no son of his was going to marry a cheap little slut who it was well-known was happy to give herself to any boy in the district who asked her!

'Of course I posted it!' she bit out derisively. 'And you received it, too!'

'How can you be so sure of that?' he challenged.

She looked away, feeling no desire to bring his dead father into all of this. 'I just know, that's all,' she insisted stubbornly.

'All right...' He held his temper with effort. 'So, let's suppose that there was a letter, and you posted it, as you are so certain you did, then—has it ever occurred to you that I may not have received it?'

'No.' Her tense mouth pursed in her certainty. Jay looked at her as though he couldn't quite believe that any of this was happening.

'Think about it, Rebecca,' he urged her patiently. 'When, in all the years we had known one another, did I ever let you down?'

'You're my knight in shining armour, and I am your damsel forever in distress!' The echo of her own carefree voice rippled through her, and pained tears filled her eyes as she saw herself, a young and happy sixteen-year-old, being lifted down from the top of a loose stone wall too high for her to jump from and too dangerous for her to have scrambled on to in the first place.

'When are you ever going to grow up and stop frightening the life out of me, Rebecca? Don't you know by now how vital you are to my very existence?'

It had been wrong—the whole thing had been wrong from the very beginning. Their coming together as lovers. The ensuing consequences which brought with it more problems and disillusionments than Rebecca had known could exist at one time.

But she should not have gone away. She knew that now with a certainty which came with the maturing of years. And Jay should have been forced to face up to his responsibilities instead of letting his father sort the mess out for him.

'I'm sorry,' she said, coming stiffly to her feet. Her heart hardened against him all over again. 'But I don't believe you. And in the end it doesn't really matter either way, because the time to put things right has gone—long gone,' she emphasised wearily. 'We may have made a child between us, Jay. But you are not really his father, and, as far as Kit is concerned, he has done well enough up until now without you. He'll survive without ever having to know you.'

'Oh, you think that, do you?' Smoothly, like a cat on the prowl, he came to his feet, his eyes like two dark slits in his suddenly ruthless face. 'Then let me tell you, you selfish little bitch, that *my* son will know his father all right!' He grabbed her arms, pulling her against him to push his face close up to hers so she had no choice but to see the force of his intent written in his eyes. 'You owe me ten years of his life! Ten damned years! And I'll have them back, damn you! Every single one of them, and *my* son will be here, living with me within the week! And you can go to the very devil for all I care!'

If the threat wasn't enough to send her tumbling into a vortex of blind panic, then the kiss he thrust cruelly upon her lips was. He crushed her slender body to him, his arms like two clamps around her while his hands buried themselves in the long, loose swathe of her hair, holding her head rigid for the violent ravaging of his kiss.

'Don't...' she whimpered when he lifted his mouth for a brief moment. 'Please don't...'

'Why not?' he taunted harshly. 'You used to glory in my kisses, delve into them with all the passion you could muster.' His lips brushed delicately across her own, sending a stinging jolt of awareness bristling through her. 'It can't have just died like that; I don't believe it.'

His mouth came down on to hers again, hard and angrily coaxing, demanding that response he was so sure was still there, hiding in the embers of her dark repressions. And almost immediately she felt those embers begin to stir, catch light as his mouth moved, back and forth, back and forth, drawing the flame, urging it, sensing its struggle for full burning life, his hands rhythmically massaging her warm and sensitive scalp.

She swayed, her body arching of its own accord into the hardening length of his, and Jay groaned something deep in his throat, dark heat striking along his cheekbones, and suddenly, trembling himself, he deepened the kiss, carrying her, protesting, back through the years to a time when this had been all she lived for.

'Please, Jay,' she begged as he slid his moist lips across her cheek to find the throbbing pulse by her lobe, 'don't do this to me again!'

'Do you think I want to feel like this?' he ground out, using his hands to tilt her head back so he could see the glow of want in her lovely wretched eyes. 'You've committed the worst crime a woman can commit against a man by withholding the knowledge of his own son from him! But, God help me, I still want you, Rebecca—have wanted you since I watched you walk towards me on that train station, looking so cool and prim it stirred my

loins into fire because I knew what a lie that façade was!'
The heat of his angry breath scored her face, sending
her eyes flickering shut on a wave of helpless pleasure.
'And this . . .' his dark voice roughened as he brought
his mouth down touching close to hers '. . . is going to
be your only saving grace, Rebecca. Keep me wanting
you and I'll let you keep your son. Otherwise I shall take
him from you! And you will never seen him again!'

The brutality of his threat beat cruelly down on her,
and she whimpered, knowing that he meant every word;
that he could do it, too. Jay had the power and the money
to take Kit away from her—even without justice on his
side. And Kit: could he lure Kit with promises of all the
things little boys yearned to own but rarely got? She knew
her son's vulnerabilities, and the worst one was not
having a father like the rest of his friends had.

'I shall always hate you for this!' she cried, fighting
desperately against the tormenting clouds of passion as
he kept up his sensual assault on her lips.

'Then hate me,' he accepted grimly. 'Because not even
if you live to be a hundred will you ever despise me as
much as I despise you right now!'

He took her mouth properly then, swinging her away
on the punishing force of his sensuality that stopped
almost as soon as it began.

'Get your coat,' he said, while she just stood there
swaying, staring at him through huge, bewildered eyes.
He was already picking up his own coat, swinging his
shoulders into it, looking like a man bent on a mission
to hell and determined not to be swayed from his course.

'B-but . . .' She licked her hot, throbbing lips, the
lingering taste of him sweet on her tongue, and she
quivered, blinking, trying to pull herself together. 'But
where are we going?' she asked him anxiously, not
understanding him, his sudden swing in mood, not understanding anything any more.

'We're going to get my son,' he told her grimly.

Rebecca came down to earth with a bump. 'But, Jay!' she cried. 'We can't drive all the way to London tonight! Look at the weather! We won't get further than the bottom of the drive! For pity's sake...' She went to grasp his arm, pulling him around to face her. 'Tomorrow!' she pleaded huskily, something in the wildness of his eyes making her gentle her tone. He was still in shock, she realised, not thinking clearly. 'The snow might have eased tomorrow, and by then the gritters will have been out clearing the roads. Please!' she urged. 'Leave it until tomorrow!'

He looked at her, listened while she made her anxious plea, then said flatly, 'Get your coat, Rebecca,' unswayed, determined, perhaps even a little mad.

CHAPTER EIGHT

AND a kind of madness it must have been which drove them out into that white treacherous night. It took them two hours just to reach the motorway. And neither of them spoke a solitary word as Jay drove with the grim concentration of one determined to reach his goal no matter what the elements wanted to throw at him, while Rebecca sat beside him, too afraid to speak, her eyes stinging with the effort it required to keep them glued on the thick slippery road, her heart in her mouth most of the time, watching, listening, feeling for the slightest jarring in the car's thick rubbered wheels which would mean they were going to start sliding into a spin, or worse perhaps, get stuck altogether.

By the time they reached the motorway she was weak with exhaustion, but at least the snow seemed to have been kept at bay on the wide, straight spread of roadway ahead of them, and at last she was able to relax her guard a little, and sink into her own troubled thoughts.

Jay's persistent denial of knowing anything about her letter confused her—because it served no useful purpose now, not unless he was solely bent on saving face. But somehow she didn't believe it was that. In the past the Jay she used to know had always stood up to his misdemeanours, large or small, taking his punishment like the man his father had been rearing him to be. So her letter, if he had received it, should have brought him racing home on the next plane. Reluctant or not, the Jay she had once believed him to be would still have come.

Could she have done him a great injustice over all these years by not at least trying to contact him a second time? She remembered being tempted on several occasions when the going had got rough and she was feeling particularly alone and afraid of what the future held for her.

But pride had stopped her, she recalled. The kind of pride which had sent her off with his father's cheque clutched tightly in her hand, ready—determined—to use every penny in it to make a kind of home for his rejected grandson.

'My son rang me today. He seems rather distressed about a letter from you in which you are making certain claims on him.'

Oh, she'd always been thoroughly intimidated by Jay's harsh and autocratic father. He was the only person she could recall who had ever had such a crushing effect on her. And that time was no different. Now, thinking back, she knew his ability to daunt her came from his rigid adherence to the lines drawn by social standards. He was of the old school, stern and Victorian in his ways. A man who did not fraternise with his staff—or condone his son's consistently doing so. He had disapproved of Jay's friendship with her, and wholeheartedly encouraged his friendship with Olivia. It didn't matter to him what went beneath the mantles of wealth or working class. Olivia was socially acceptable, and Rebecca was not. It really was as simple as that.

So, to have been hauled up in front of him that awful morning was as though she were being hauled up to face a hanging judge, so easily had he crushed her spirit.

'My son, of course, denies it all.'

She hadn't even thought of questioning that statement. She'd just trembled and stammered something about, 'But I'm telling the truth, sir.' She always had called him sir: her mother had drummed it into her since she had been a mere babe in arms. 'He's the master and we treat him with respect.' And she had, with a deferring respect which had sent her own self-esteem to rock-bottom level when she was in his company.

'When it's well-known that half the young men in this area have helped themselves to you?'

Blank-brained, stunned by the accusation, she'd just stood there staring at him, frightened out of her wits and trying desperately to understand who could have told him such a terrible lie! She had received her answer without having to ask for it.

'My son is rather sceptical, Rebecca, whether you would know who is the actual father of your child—if there is a child, that is. That isn't just another little lie you've trumped up to try to trap him, is it?'

Slowly, carefully, so as not to alert Jay to her movement, she turned her head to study him. He was still pale in the face, his features drawn and grim. But the attraction was still there, emanating through the veils of strain. Ten years ago that face had used to crack with impulsive smiles, with no reason for them, just the sudden turning of his head and the grin which said, 'I'm happy. I love being with you.' She hadn't seen him smile much since she'd come back, hardly at all really, and never that particular smile, the warm and carefree one.

Life had a way of doing that, she supposed—taking the impulsiveness out of the boy. She didn't smile much herself when she came to think of it, whereas once, in Jay's company, she would never stop—they would never stop—laughing, teasing, fighting, loving ... The pain of remembrance began spreading throughout her body, recognition of the kind of love and trust they once used to share.

Would that Jay she used to know—or even this one now—turn his back on his responsibilities? She only had to see him with her mother to know, deep down in her heart, that it wasn't so. Had she been a fool to believe his father? A blind, stupid, frightened fool to believe that Jay would desert her as callously as that?

She shivered, pulling the warm collar of her coat higher around her throat. There was no other way his father could have known about her pregnancy unless it had come from Jay's own lips. Because she had not told anybody else, waiting anxiously for his reply, or, more hopefully, his sudden appearance when he would scoop her up into his arms and tell her not to worry, he was here now, and everything would be all right.

No; she told her mind to stop looking for excuses for Jay. There were none. They did not exist.

The car sped on, stopping once to refill the petrol tank, and Jay came back with a cup of hot coffee for her, acquired via one of those awful vending machines which specialised in polystyrene drinks. But she accepted it gratefully, having not eaten or drunk a single thing since she'd shared a light lunch with her mother.

Her mother...

The car was set into motion again, with no word exchanged between them, the mood still black and heavy, and she watched the whitened countryside slide swiftly by, the soft growl of the car engine and the faint hiss of rubber on the wet tarmacadam road surface somehow soothing.

She would have liked to call the hospital and check on her mother, but the mere idea of making the suggestion to this grim-faced and totally withdrawn man beside her intimidated her almost as much as his father had used to do.

Calling to enquire about her mother would have to wait until they reached home—her home. Hers and Kit's home. Not Jay's, never Jay's, and perhaps not Kit's soon either, if Jay's hard determination to eke revenge on her maintained its present course.

She shivered again, and he turned to glance at her. 'Cold?' he said. She shook her head, not wanting to speak, and looked away, out of the side window. The silence fell between them again, and she was glad of it. She really had nothing more to say to Jay. Nothing.

She dozed for a time, half asleep but half alert, aware of the car's smooth running movement, of Jay, large and grim beside her, of the silent passing of mile upon mile until she sat up suddenly, some sixth sense telling her they had reached the built-up outskirts of London itself.

'Where now?' he asked, not looking at her this time, but keeping his eyes fixed on the road. He looked exhausted, hollow-eyed.

She told him in a dull, flat tone which part of London to make for, then fell silent again until he required more instruction.

The snow hadn't reached this far, turning to rain in the heat emanating from the big city, the roads and pavements soaked and gleaming golden in the misty lamp-light. She directed him into the road where she lived, indicating which house he was to pull up outside, then, opening her door, Rebecca clambered out on legs gone dead from the hours of inactivity.

Jay joined her on the pavement, big and looming. A man on a mission, his face still wearing that closed and uncompromising grimness.

'Kit isn't here,' she thought it best to inform him as she placed her key in the front-door lock. 'He's staying with friends.'

Jay nodded, having probably already worked that out for himself. In the narrow hallway she switched on the light, aware of him behind her, shouldering in through the door and closing it securely. She moved sluggishly for the stairs, too done-in to think much further than a hot drink and her bed, but Jay's voice stopped her.

'I would appreciate a drink before we try to sleep, Rebecca,' he said, the request sounding as if it killed him to make it.

She turned, eyeing him in the harsh, unflattering light from the overhead bulb. He looked dreadful. 'The kitchen is upstairs,' she told him. 'The rooms down here are given up to my factory.'

A dark eyebrow arched at her, but he said nothing, though she sensed the critical thoughts going on in his head—all to do with Kit, and how utterly unsatisfactory he believed it to be to bring up a child in such conditions. They were happy here, she and Kit, but, too tired to state the point just now, she led the way up the stairs without a word, glad the house had not lain empty while she had been away. The girls' coming in and working here meant the heating had been on, and so it wasn't too cold.

The kitchen was what once had been the tiny boxroom of her four-bedroomed house. The largest bedroom was now the sitting-room, and the other two her and Kit's bedrooms. She walked into the kitchen and turned on the light, wincing because it was fluorescent and hurt her eyes more than the ordinary bulb in the hall downstairs had done.

The kettle waited, filled and ready to switch on, a strict routine, which was part of every working day, being that Rebecca's home was left neat and tidy when she was away on a business trip.

'Tea or coffee?' she asked him.

He was pulling out a chair at her kitchen table, his coat already lying over the back of another chair. 'Tea,' he replied. 'Coffee will only keep me awake.' He sat down wearily, and rubbed his face with a hand. 'How far away is he?'

She had sensed that all through the journey Jay's thoughts had been honed exclusively on Kit, and that question confirmed it, or he would have used his son's name.

'Not far.' She placed the required tea-bags into the old-fashioned earthenware pot while she waited for the kettle to boil. 'A ten-minute car drive away, no more.'

He nodded, too physically exhausted to do more. 'I'll go and collect him in the morning.'

'No!' Rebecca jerked around, fear striking up from deep inside her. 'Y-you don't have to do that. Ch-Christina will be bringing him here with her in the morning,' she rushed on unsteadily. 'They'll be here for nine o'clock. So it would be silly your going to collect him.'

Jay nodded, and she wilted against the unit with relief that he had taken her advice. There was no way she could just let Jay announce his appearance in Kit's life like that. It was just too brutal.

'Here,' she said, 'drink your tea,' and placed a steaming mug in front of him. 'Then we'll try to get some sleep.'

'What time is it?' He sounded punch-drunk, his eyes lost in their hollowed sockets.

'One-thirty,' she told him, glancing at the kitchen clock. The place would be alive with people by nine, she thought drily. God knew how she was going to manage to face them all in this state.

She sat down across from him, hugging her own drink in her hands while she sipped wearily at it. Jay did the same, staring at the shiny white laminate table, the silence between them possessing a dull throb.

'What the hell happened to us, Becky?' he murmured suddenly, lifting his bloodshot eyes to meet hers. 'Where the hell did we go wrong?'

Tears filled her eyes. 'I don't know, Jay,' she whispered huskily. 'I never did really know.'

'God,' he groaned, hunching over his hot drink. 'The whole damned thing is going round and round in my head until I can barely see straight, never mind think!'

'Then don't try,' she suggested wearily, then took pity on him because the whole thing was such an utter mess. She reached out to touch his hand. 'It's useless to keep going over and over it all. Leave the rest until tomorrow, until your mind has been given a chance to think more clearly.'

His hand turned in hers, his dark head hunched and lowered on his wide shoulders as he watched his fingers measure their long lean length against her own smaller, finer-boned ones, and Rebecca bit down hard on her bottom lip, the tears in her eyes growing hot as another wave of aching sympathy for him washed over her. No matter what had happened ten years ago, she at least had it in her to acknowledge that Jay had missed out on the most fulfilling experience of his life by rejecting his son. And perhaps, she concluded heavily, like her mother, Jay had been living with his own brand of guilt, and the only way he had been able to deal with it was by shoving it all away, denying even to himself that any of the blame was his own. After all, she tagged on ruefully to that last thought, wasn't that exactly what she had done herself? Thrust them all out of her mind because she couldn't bear to think about what they had done to her and Kit?

'Come on,' she sighed, sliding her hand from his, 'Let's go to bed. You can use Kit's room since he isn't here,' she offered awkwardly.

'No.' His dark head shook, that grim resolve coming back into his red-rimmed eyes. 'We sleep in the same bed for what's left of tonight.'

The announcement sent her shooting back in her seat, and she stared at him as if he'd just asked her to slit her own throat. 'I'm not sleeping with you!' she cried, wondering dizzily if indeed he had gone mad.

'You are,' he insisted immovably, 'or you won't sleep at all. There is no way, Rebecca, I am going to give you a chance to sneak out of here in the middle of the night to steal my son away from me a second time!'

'But—that's crazy thinking, Jay!' she gasped, looking at him through wide bewildered eyes. 'Where would I go? My home is here . . . my work! You're not thinking clearly,' she excused his momentary aberration and stood up, turning to leave the room. 'Use Kit's bed, and I'll wake you in time to——'

'I said we sleep together,' he reiterated grimly. 'God knows...' he sighed, 'I need a bit of human comfort tonight, and I don't see why it shouldn't be you who provides it, since it's you who's filled me with all this bloody wretchedness I'm feeling right now!' Again the hot eyes pierced her, and she flinched from the bitter accusations written there. 'Sleep,' he made quite cuttingly clear, 'that's all I'm expecting, just in case your twisted mind is working overtime on my motives. Sleep, with the security of knowing I have you clamped safely to my side before I have to face him in the morning!'

Rebecca sighed, her shoulders drooping wearily in defeat. 'Sleep,' she conceded heavily, just too tired to battle with him any more tonight. Then, before she could allow herself to think about what she was giving in to, she walked out of the room, Jay couldn't know it, but she was desperate for a bit of that human comfort herself. A need she had not felt for so many years that it felt strange yet peculiarly right somehow that it should be him to give it her—however obliquely given.

'The bathroom is through there.' She pointed to a door to her left. 'I'll—change, while you wash.'

It took her only a few minutes to discard her clothes in exchange for a soft silky nightdress and a warm wrap which she hugged around herself while she waited for Jay to finish with the bathroom. They passed in the doorway, their eyes careful not to collide. When she came back he was lying beneath the duvet, his eyes closed, face drawn with weariness.

Slipping off her wrap, she slid in beside him, trying to be very careful not to brush against him, unsure if he was wearing anything and suspecting not.

His arm snaked out and gathered her close, moulding her slender frame into the muscled curve of his. 'Thank you for this,' he murmured sleepily into the silky cloud of her hair. 'I know it was an imposition, but I needed you tonight, Becky, I needed you...'

He dropped into sleep that quickly, gone in a single blink of an eye. Rebecca lay tensely in his arms for a while, not quite believing it had happened just like that, listening to his steady breathing, feeling the warm brush of his breath on her exposed nape; then, slowly, she began to relax, warmed by his body pressed against the back of her own, slowly dragged down by the tiredness pulling at her eyes, and she slept too.

For how long she had no idea, but she came awake slowly, aware of a delicious warmth invading her body, the kind of liquid warmth that made her stretch languidly, then settle back on a silky sigh.

Jay watched the telling movements from his position, raised on one elbow, his torso half leaning over her while his eyes ran over her sleep-softened features. She was smiling a little, enjoying the gentle stroke of his hand against her belly above the thin, silky fabric of her nightdress. He bent down to brush her cheek with his lips, and she murmured something, turning a little in dreamy search for more.

He gave it, kissing her small nose, her satin-smooth brows, the creamy lids of her closed eyes, and the soft scented flush on her cheeks.

'Becky...' he murmured softly.

'Jay...' she sighed, and turned fully into him, her arm coming up to wind languidly around his neck, holding him to her, her body arching and flexing in the age-old movement of growing desire.

He smiled to himself—nothing sinister, just a gentle smile that suited the gentle way she was coming awake, then he lowered his mouth again, finding her lips, slightly parted and softened ready for him, and slowly, sensually, he began drawing her closer to the surface of consciousness, his hand moving on her body, arousing her, lazily drawing the fine covering of her nightdress along her silken legs and further up to her hips.

Rebecca came awake as his hand slid gently between her thighs. 'Jay!' she gasped, still not sure if she were dreaming or not, the muzzy clouds of sleep taking their time to disperse.

'Ssh,' he murmured, 'it's all right. You want me, Becky, your body is telling me so, and God knows...' he whispered shakily, 'I want you...'

His mouth covered hers again, cutting off any protest she might have wanted to make. And, while she struggled with her own growing need to just stop thinking and let this happen, he began to stroke her, surely and knowingly, stalling the air inside her lungs as the white-hot flame of desire began licking pleasurably through her.

Oh, no... She whimpered deep down inside as it all began to stir—her body, her heart and her poor hungry soul. And already she knew she was lost, moving to a rhythm Jay had created in her long ago, and knew just how to make the magic flow again.

'I don't want this,' she groaned on a shaken cry as he moved his upper torso over her, the crisp dark hair on his chest rasping against the aroused and sensitive tips of her breasts.

'Of course you do,' he assured. 'It was what you were born for, to be mine like this.'

Was she? Had she been born to know only the magical beauty of this man's touch? As she lay there, being stroked into breathless subjugation by his sensual touch, she could believe it, for no other man had ever been this close to her. No other man had ever been Jay.

'You'll kill me with this, do you know that?' she cried as despair of what she was letting happen made her put up a final struggle.

'But what a way to die, my darling,' he murmured whimsically. 'Lost in the arms of the man you crave—as he craves you, desperately, fatally. God, Rebecca, but you have to touch me; this is all such sweet, sweet torment!'

She awoke to the languid knowledge that something radical had changed in her life. Turning on to her back, she stretched lithely, sinking back into the warm covers with a contented smile playing about her lips.

Then she was still, the accidental movement of her hand meeting with warm and naked human flesh, sending her into a moment's paralysis of shock. Then she turned her head, saw Jay's dark one sleeping peacefully next to her, and remembrance came flooding back with a dark flush of horror staining her cheeks.

'God in heaven!' she breathed, too stunned to do anything but stare at him. What had she done?

He looked relaxed and contented, more like the Jay she used to know with the layers of cynicism wiped away from his face. Her heart flipped, then settled into a quivering lump in her breast. And tears, mourning what had once been, slid silently from her eyes.

She loved him, she accepted achingly. Totally and irrevocably, she loved, had loved, and always would love him. And the knowledge left her feeling bleak and lonely, because she now knew that, no matter what Jay threw at her in the way of pain and grief, he could never kill her feelings for him, because they were such a strong and innate part of her being.

And maybe that was why she'd run away all those years ago. Not because his father had frightened her into it. And not because her mother had supported everything Cedric Lorence had said. But because Jay had denounced her, and she knew that she would never be able to come face to face with his rejection and survive it.

Did that mean she would allow him to inflict any kind of pain on her and always manage to forgive him? Probably, she accepted with the bitter taste of self-condemnation filling her mouth.

His eyes flicked open, bright shining blue revealing instant recall.

'Why?' she demanded.

He smiled, not even trying to misunderstand her, and hauled himself up on to his elbow to look mockingly down on her. 'I want my son,' he said simply. 'At any price, but preferably by the easiest route possible. You are that route, Rebecca. Through the mother I gain the son.' He reached out to touch a fingertip to the corner of her soft mouth, his eyes drawn down to watch the uncontrollable way her lips quivered for him, and he smiled with dry satisfaction.

'You—you planned this?' she said, appalled that he could be so cunningly ruthless.

'What do you think I was doing on that long journey down here?' His eyes flicked up to mock her. 'Plotting your quick demise?' Her look said that that was exactly what she had thought he was doing, and he smiled wryly. 'I'm not a fool, Rebecca, though I know you damned well think me one. The gentlest way to gain my son is through you. You have to be on my side to make his acceptance of me easier—for both of us.'

She frowned, not understanding. 'I don't see how seducing me gains you that support.'

'Of course you do!' he mocked her gently, smiling lazily down at her as he sent his hand on an exploratory sweep of her body. Instantly she was gasping, the flick of heated fire sending her arching up to meet that hand, and Jay laughed triumphantly. 'See!' he taunted. 'Mine, Rebecca! I only have to touch you like this...' he did it again, and again she responded helplessly '...to have you willing to do anything for the love of my body!'

'God!' she choked, shutting her eyes to block out the cruel triumphant sight of him. She was sinking dizzyingly, tumbling down into the hot flaming mass of her own damning desire. 'I hate you!'

'But you're ready for me,' he informed her cruelly, and rolled himself on top of her, parting her thighs and thrusting his way into her body with a ruthless intent which made her cry out in shocked delight of it. 'Say it, Rebecca!' he demanded roughly, his dark face hard and determined, mere inches from her own. He gave a hard thrust with his hips, and she cried out again, welcoming him. 'Say it. I want to hear you say it!'

'Say what?' she whimpered wretchedly.

He thrust again, and she welcomed him again with another shameful cry. 'You know, you little torment. Say it, damn you, or I swear I'll play you like this until you die from the frustration of it!'

He thrust again, and she arched violently beneath him. 'I want you, Jay!' she cried, her hands sliding tormentedly up his strong arms, fingers curling tightly into the bunched muscles in his shoulders. 'I want you,' she repeated huskily.

'How much?'

'How much do you want me, Becky?'

'All of me. All of me wants you, Jay!'

'All of me!' she cried out desperately. 'All of me wants you!'

The surrendering act of saying the words brought a surge of self-contempt flaming through her, and she opened her eyes, the impassioned grey alight with need and hatred. She read the triumph glinting in his eyes, and his own mix of need and hatred, and on a husky animal growl dug in her nails and drew them scoringly down his chest.

He cried out, arching on the pain of it, and shuddered, his body swelling inside her, aroused, inflaming him to a height of angry desire which exalted her because it showed that Jay was no less vulnerable to her firebrand kind of passion than she was to his.

'You little hell cat!' he grated, searing her with his eyes. Then he laughed, the younger Jay rising through the ashes of the older one to reach out and twist her flying hair into a hard and imprisoning knot, holding her head arching backwards against the pillows so that his mouth could come down hot on her exposed throat, honing in on and biting the wild throbbing pulse-point where her neck met with her smooth silky shoulder.

Then, as the pulsing rhythm of their bodies threatened to throw them off the edge of the world, he murmured hoarsely, 'My God, how have I lived without this for so damned long?'

How have I? she wondered hazily, saddened, even while he exalted her senses, saddened by it all.

She lay, too weak to do much more than watch him through languid, sleepy lids as he moved around her small bedroom, so completely unaware of his own disturbing attraction that she smiled.

His long legs were superbly corded with strong lithe muscle, his flanks tight and slim, his waist spare of any hint of unnecessary flesh. And the long lean shape of his body ran upwards in smooth muscled lines, spreading outwards to accommodate his steel-hard chest covered liberally with crisp dark hair, and the wide rippling stretch of his silken shoulders. Ten years ago Jay's body had been a wonderful sight to see naked like this. Now it had gained in maturity, toned out, fined down, and become the perfect vision of man.

He turned, catching her studying him, his blue eyes sharpening on her slender supine figure flushed with the marks of his loving. 'You're mine now, Rebecca,' he stated tersely. 'Remember that when Kit comes home. It could mean the difference between your keeping or losing him.'

'Don't threaten me, Jay,' she said quietly, too lazy to let him rile her to anger. And, anyway, she had already accepted—way back into last night—that she was his, had been and always would be his. Even when he no longer wanted her... 'You haven't altered much over the years, have you?' she put in ruefully. 'Still a damned hell of a figure of a man!'

He smiled, as if he couldn't help himself, and came to lean over her on the bed. 'Neither have you, my bitter torment,' he murmured, and dropped a lingering kiss on her welcoming lips. 'And I have the marks to prove it,' he added drily as he pulled away, drawing her eyes along the two lines of red finger-marks running down his hair-roughened chest to the concave wall of his stomach.

Her eyes flicked back to his, not even the faintest hint of remorse in their defiant grey depths. And he laughed softly, shaking his dark head, then touched a finger to the side of her neck where it felt sore and faintly bruised. 'But I've left my mark on you too, my lovely,' he informed her smugly, laughing again when she gasped, her hand jumping up to where he had just mockingly touched. 'They used to call them love-bites, but I prefer to think of that one as my personal brand—step out of line from now on, Rebecca,' he warned, 'and I shall just show that to whoever is about, and see how that rather impressive façade of cool authority you've developed during the years drops revealingly away.'

He kissed her again, a quick kiss, hard with resolve, then moved away from her. 'Get up,' he said. 'I don't want my son arriving here to find his mother lying in bed waiting for her lover to return to her.'

'You're a bastard, Jay, you really are,' she murmured drily as she forced herself to move, then went still when he turned angrily on her.

'I'm not, but my son is,' he bit out grimly. 'A mistake which will be put right at the first damned opportunity I get!'

'What's that supposed to mean?' she demanded, alarmed.

'Get up,' he repeated, refusing to discuss the subject further. 'I'll go and make a drink.'

And he'd gone, leaving Rebecca staring at the empty doorway, chewing on her lower lip, wondering just how many plans Jay had made during that long grim journey from Yorkshire last night.

CHAPTER NINE

'THEY'RE here.' Rebecca watched from the window Christina's car draw up behind Jay's, and her son clamber quickly out to go hunting around the body of the low, powerful black monster, chatting ten to the dozen to Christina about the car's famous shape and style, his familiar voice high-pitched with awe.

Jay shot out of his chair, the tension in him so bad that it vibrated in the air around him. They had been waiting like this for half an hour now, the passionate intimacy of the night before gone as quickly as it had flared, leaving them stiffly formal, coolly remote, lost behind the impenetrable masks of their own tense thoughts.

Christina had already moved out of sight, standing right beneath Rebecca's window while she fished for her front-door key. She made some joking remark, mocking the child's envious tones, and Kit turned to look at her, his young face smiling ruefully. Then he caught sight of Rebecca standing in the first-floor window, and the smile split into a warm grin of surprise.

'Mum!' he shouted, and her heart shot, trembling, to her stomach as he sent her a quick wave then came galloping towards the front door.

'Please, Jay...' She turned urgently from the window, anxiety for Kit, and what Jay was about to do, forcing her to plead with him. 'Let me speak to him alone first—explain!'

'Explain how?' he grimly challenged. 'By sitting him down and telling him what a careless rat he has for a father before introducing me?' He lifted his eyes to her, paled to a hard determined silver. 'No.' He turned his back on her, the shoulders beneath his dark business suit uncompromising. 'We do this together,' he clipped immovably.

'But——' The front door was already open, and she could hear Christina's sharp surprised voice questioning Kit's certainty that his mother was actually here, and Rebecca stepped quickly forwards, going to place a trembling hand on his arm. 'You're his father, for God's sake, Jay!' she pleaded anxiously. 'I couldn't hurt him by painting you black! It would mean I was painting him black also!'

The quick sound of small feet clattering up the stairs stopped the air inside her lungs, and the pressure inside her began to buzz in her ears as she turned a little wildly, already knowing it was too late. Jay turned too, standing beside her to face the door, his silvered eyes fixed on it, tension throbbing from him, the pair of them unaware of the way Rebecca clutched in agitation at his arm. Then the door flew open, and Kit was standing there, his young face alight with pleasure.

'Mum!' he panted breathlessly. 'When did you get back? Have you seen that smashing Ferrari parked outside our house? Who do you think...?' His voice trailed off, his gaze at last seeing the tall dark stranger standing beside his mother, and the excitement bubbling from him faded into guarded awkwardness. 'Oh,' he said, 'sorry. I didn't realise you had someone with you.'

Then silence held the room in its thrall. Nothing— nothing of the million and one ways she had envisaged this meeting happening over the years coming anywhere near the true and devastating reality of it, as Jay stood staring at the paralysing sight of himself recreated in the younger image of his son.

Then Christina came up behind Kit, breaking the high-tensile moment, her pretty face curious as she gazed into the room over the top of Kit's motionless head. Rebecca glanced appealingly at her, and shook her head in mute warning, the tears in her eyes and the strain obvious in her paste-white face enough to alert Christina that something momentous was about to take place. Her eyes shifted to Jay, and, as it would be with anyone who knew Kit, the recognition was instant, and her own face paled as she flicked her shocked glance back to Rebecca. Then, with a sensitivity Rebecca would thank her for later, she nodded and turned away, quietly going back down the stairs to leave them alone again.

'Kit...' By necessity, Rebecca pulled herself together, unclipping her locked fingers from Jay's arm and swallowing before she could stretch her lips into a semblance of her usual welcoming smile for her son. 'Come here,' she urged him huskily, reaching out an inviting hand towards him. 'I have someone here who wants to meet you...'

Kit took the hand, allowing himself to be drawn to his mother's side, his wary gaze barely flickering from Jay's taut, still face.

Struggling to maintain some control over her own emotions in this highly emotive moment, Rebecca turned her son to stand in front of her, her hands resting on his thin little shoulders, then lifted her anguished eyes to Jay's.

'Jay...' she murmured huskily, having to speak through a heaving barrier of tears, 'this is Kit. Kit,' she said very gently to her son, 'this is—an old friend of mine. H-his name is Jason Lorence, and he is...' She couldn't say it; the words just would not come out, and her mouth began to tremble, the corners turning down as she struggled for composure, appealing to Jay for mercy, for help, for some sign from him as to how she was supposed to rock her own son's life in such a harsh unprepared way.

'Hello,' Kit said, taking the initiative away from both adults by holding out his hand towards his father, unaware of what yet was to come crashing down on his head. Just curious, sensing the tension in the atmosphere, not understanding it, but respecting it with his grave, polite little voice.

Jay didn't move, seemingly incapable of doing so, and Rebecca looked anxiously at him. If she had thought him white-faced a moment or so earlier, he was ashen now, the tension in him driven to a point where it was obvious he was labouring under the severest kind of shock.

'Jay...' she appealed unsteadily to him, and a wave of bitter sympathy washed through her at the way his eyes flickered then slid up to clash blankly with hers. She grimaced, the tiniest involuntary shrug of her shoulders telling him she just didn't know how else to bridge the final gap between him and his son, and he looked away without acknowledgement, fixing his gaze back on Kit's watchful face.

The child moved, uncomfortable beneath the un-blinking stare, and the small hand he held out wavered, wanting to drop away but Kit not sure whether he should let it or not. The slight moving of the hand brought Jay's attention to it, and he stood for a moment looking at that instead of Kit's face, then back at the face, then back at the hand, and his own came up, slowly and shakily, to close around the little boy's.

Then he was lifting his eyes back to Rebecca, hard accusation in their silver depths. This is my son! those bitter eyes were telling her. Mine! In every way that matters, and you'll pay for keeping him hidden from me!

She shuddered, having to look away, pain and guilt filling her until she felt like weeping. She heard Jay drag in a long unsteady breath, pulling himself together; then he said huskily, 'Hello, son,' and that possessive 'son' ripped at Rebecca's possessive heart, making her want to lash out at something—anything—to rid herself of

the terrible wave of violence which suddenly overwhelmed her.

'Is that your car outside?' Kit asked curiously, encouraged by the man's smile. 'It's a Ferrari, isn't it? I
know because I've seen a picture of one in a book. How
fast does it go? Does it go over a hundred? My mum's
car will only do seventy, and only then when we're on
the motorway, but...'

The barrage of light, quick chatter sent another breath
of air into Jay's lungs, bringing him surer and surer back
from the stunned dark place that shock had sent him
away to.

'It certainly is,' he replied. 'And if you like I'll take
you for a spin in it later.'

'Would you?' Kit's eyes went wide, and he took an
eager step away from Rebecca, dislodging her hands,
unknowingly taking his very first step away from his
mother to the father he had never known. 'That would
be great! I've never been out in a car like that before!'
Awe and excitement filled his voice, and Rebecca reeled
stiffly away, her hands going to clasp each other tightly
beneath her breasts where her heart raced, pummelling
at the tight wall of her chest.

'But later, though,' Jay made clear before the small
boy was overwhelmed with eagerness. 'First,' he went
on more seriously, 'we—that is, your mother and I—
have something important we want to tell you...'

Rebecca went perfectly still, her nerve-ends beginning
to prickle, knowing what was about to come. Jay was
not going to let any of them leave this room until the
full truth had been told to Kit.

'Rebecca.' Jay called her name, quietly, but firmly
enough to have her turning back to face him, her body
locked in the trembling morass of her own painful
emotions as, for one last time, she appealed to him with
her eyes.

His hand came out, his clear blue gaze denying the plea, silently commanding her to come to his side, join him in what he was about to do, face it, face it all with him.

She swallowed, and dropped her gaze from his, moving on stiff limbs over to him, tensing even more as he slid that outstretched hand around her waist and drew her against his side. Then he was looking back at his son, studying the curious way Kit had watched this little display of intimacy.

Then he said gravely and very formally, 'I want to marry your mother, Kit. But she insists we have to have your agreement first.'

Rebecca's world tilted on its axis, the complete and shocking unexpectedness of his words knocking the sense right out of her, and she swayed in the arc of Jay's arm. His grip tightened in warning, his gaze never leaving their son as suddenly and belligerently he glared at them both and demanded, 'Why?' his youth and innocence allowing the almost rude enquiry to leave his lips.

Jay's smile was rueful. 'Because she's the only woman in this world I've ever wanted to marry,' he answered rather drily. 'And,' he added, while Rebecca waited, eyes closed and trembling, for the last hammer to fall, 'because I love her very much, and she loves me.'

'Do you?' Kit's aggressive little challenge brought her eyes flickering open to find him glaring at her with his cheeks running red with anger.

'I . . .' She couldn't answer, found herself incapable of saying anything sensible. Jay had thoroughly disconcerted her with what he had said, knocked her so clean off balance that she didn't even know if she was angry or relieved by the cunning way he was tackling all of this.

Another of his clever plans drawn up while they'd shared that long, cold, silent journey home? 'Through the mother, I gain the son,' he had told her only hours before while she'd lain wrapped in his arms. My God! she thought, sending him a bitter look. He's a ruthless, cunning bastard!

Kit was waiting for her reply, looking at her through Jay's hard assessing eyes, and despair wafted over her, an acknowledgement that this was how Jay meant to make her pay for what he believed to be her crimes against him: through the guise of love in marriage, with total dedication to him and his son.

'Yes,' she whispered defeatedly at last, knowing that she really did not have any choice. Jay was holding out for much higher stakes than she had taken into consideration. He wanted his son, heart, body and soul, and the only way he could achieve that was by pretending an undying love for the child's mother, otherwise Kit would always be suspicious of him, never really sure why his father had ignored them both for nine long years only to come walking into his life to claim him.

'Why?' The rude question was thrown directly at her now, and Rebecca forced herself to put aside her own feelings and Jay's motives to try at least to make the poor child understand some of it.

Leaving Jay's side, she went down on her haunches in front of her son, and took hold of him gently by his shoulders. 'You remember, Kit,' she began carefully, 'years ago, when you asked me all about where I used to live and where you came from?'

He nodded grimly, his angry blue gaze fixed firmly on her pale strained face.

'And I told you that——' she swallowed tensely '—that I used to live a long way from here, and——'

'Yorkshire,' the small boy provided. 'You said you used to live in Yorkshire. That's where you've just been, isn't it? Where you met—him.' He sent the listening Jay a resentful glance.

'Yes,' his mother agreed, 'that is where I met Jay again——'

'Again?' Kit said sharply.

'No, Rebecca.' Jay's hand came down warningly on her shoulder. 'This is not the——'

'Again,' she repeated firmly, ignoring Jay, ignoring Kit's tense, suspicious face. Jay was wrong, and this was the way—the only way to get all the hurt over in one fell swoop so that the healing process could begin. 'Jay and I have known each other since we were children. We grew up together.' He her loyal champion, she his adoring slave—a smile touched her lips, wistful and wry. 'And I suppose it was only natural that eventually we should fall in love with each other... But I was very young then, Kit,' she went on huskily, 'and—and so wild that I was difficult to control...' Which was the truth, she realised now on looking back. Almost impossible to keep in hand—a constant worry to her mother—a danger unto herself. 'Jay had to go away...' she focused her eyes back on her son and away from the past '...to America to work and I h-had to leave Yorkshire to f-find a job, begin t-taking care of myself, and w-we lost touch with each other.'

'It's him—isn't it?'

Kit took a jerky step back from her, dislodging her hands, going to stand stiff and alone several feet away, his young face pale with knowledge. He glared accusingly at Rebecca.

'It's him, the one you told me about!' His eyes flicked to Jay with a bitter look, his thin young body beginning to shake. 'He's my father—isn't he?'

Another step back brought him up against the arm of a chair, and he stood, glaring at her through Jay's accusing blue eyes, hating her, and Rebecca had to glance away for a moment as anguish ripped across the shredded surface of her heart.

'But he didn't even care about us!' the child cried out angrily, his hurt, nearly ten years in the harbouring, pouring out in that hot resentful tone. He stood stiff and unapproachable, glaring from one tense adult face to the other. 'He didn't care——' a small hand flicked out in Jay's direction '—and you've let him make you love him again!'

'Of course I cared, Kit,' Jay put in huskily, taking a jerky step towards the boy only to stop when his own blue eyes flashed him a look of pure hatred.

'Not about me, you didn't,' Kit accused him.

'That is because he knew nothing about you!' Rebecca cried, and suddenly the room was thrown into silence. A complete and utter silence which held her own damnation in its naked grasp. 'I t-told you,' she went on unsteadily, 'Remember, darling—I told you how your father and I had lost touch even before you were born, so he couldn't know anything about you, could he?'

'He could have tried to find you!' the child stated wretchedly. 'If he loved you like you said, then he could have tried to find us!'

'I did try,' Jay inserted, his face taut with strain, but holding his son's sceptical gaze steady. 'I tried for years to find your mother, but she seemed to have dropped off the face of the earth! Because no one seemed to have heard or seen her since she left us.'

'Us?' Kit's brain was working so sharply that he was picking up on every innuendo offered him, greedy, in a way, for the truth, the whole unfettered truth of it.

'Me, and your grandmother,' Jay grimly confirmed. 'Your mother's mother.'

The child's eyes widened. 'I have a grandmother too?' He flicked his mother with a look of such bloody condemnation that she flinched at it.

Rebecca got stiffly to her feet, deciding that this had to be brought firmly in hand before Kit sent it whirling out of anyone's control. In all honesty, she hadn't expected him to react quite so hostilely. In these days of public enlightenment, children tended to know more about human relationships than they had done in her day. She had explained to Kit the situation between herself and his father as best she possibly could under the circumstances, years ago, when he had wanted to know, doing it without, she had hoped, showing Jay in a bad light, for Kit's sake rather than Jay's. He had known his father was alive, known that, through circumstances, that same father knew nothing about him, had seemed at the time to accept it all with a reasonable grace; but now it became heart-wrenchingly clear to Rebecca that, far from accepting, Kit had probably spent years wondering about his father, cudgelling out the whys and why nots of his continued absence from his life, coming to decisions, bleak, cruel, empty decisions which had given him the insight to shout his present accusations.

All these years, she realised guiltily, her poor son had been starving for the love of his father, and she hadn't known!

Grimly, she walked over to him, grasping him firmly by the hand, and drew him around the chair arm to sit him down beside her, her eyes searching coolly for Jay's. 'Sit down,' she told him huskily. 'Please; it will be easier for him if neither of us looms over him in any way.'

He was pale and grim. There was a moment's hesitation, when he looked as if he might challenge her right to deal with this her way, then he nodded his dark head, and went to do as she'd suggested, lowering himself carefully into the chair opposite them, to sit hunched forward, his eyes fixed concernedly on his red-faced and belligerent son.

'Listen to me, Kit,' she commanded, making him, by the firm tone of her voice, turn to look at her. 'I know this has all come as a big shock to you, but you must let me explain the full story to you before you begin to make any judgements . . .'

And quietly, calmly, Rebecca began the story at its easiest point, with the notice in the paper and her mother's illness.

'But you never even told me you had a mother!' Kit cried, accusing her all over again.

'I know...' Her fingers played restlessly with his. 'We had a row, you see, and I—ran away.'

'At the same time you ran away from him?' His dark head gave a terse nod in Jay's direction, and Rebecca saw the faint twist of cynicism touch Jay's mouth.

'Yes,' she confirmed. 'And, being such a terribly proud person, Kit, I never got in touch with either of them again.'

'And did you want to?' he asked her curiously.

Something pitiful quivered inside her. 'Oh, yes,' she sighed. She had wanted to, in those brief moments of loneliness when she had longed for either or both of them. But she hadn't believed they would want to hear from her. And that was when the pride would come looming up again, hardening her against her moment's weakness, forcing her to carry on on her own—show them all... 'Sometimes,' she murmured softly.

'Is she very poorly?'

'Yes, quite poorly,' she blinked back to the present, 'but getting a little stronger every day.' Via the telephone this morning, the hospital had told her that her mother had had a reasonable night, but they were keeping her sedated for the rest of today, just to be on the safe side.

Kit's feet shifted restlessly beside her, his black leather trainers making a scuffling noise on the plain brown carpet. 'Does she know about me?' he asked her gruffly, his young face guarded.

'Yes, she does now.' According to the hospital, the first words her mother had spoken this morning had been an announcement that she had a grandson. Rebecca smiled and squeezed his hands in reassurance. 'And wants very much to meet and get to know you.'

'But first we had to get this problem of me, and my wish to marry your mother and be the father I should be to you, out of the way,' Jay put in quietly.

And all the attention shifted to him: Kit's, Rebecca's, the room seeming to tilt sideways, aiming everything at Jay's calm smooth face.

'You know my grandmother?' he asked Jay curiously, and even Jay himself saw the rueful side of Kit's eagerness to talk about a grandmother while he shied away from discussing Jay's rights in his life.

'Jay has been looking after her for us,' Rebecca put in quietly.

'You have?' That piece of information seemed to earn Jay his first look of reluctant respect from his son. 'Will she like me, do you think?' he murmured tentatively.

Something pained swept over Jay's pale face. 'I think she will love you on sight,' he assured his son huskily. 'You look so much like your mother that she could do nothing else.'

'No, I don't,' Kit stiffly denied, the moment's warmth emptying out of his eyes. 'I look like you.' He said it almost accusingly, then glanced away from Jay again.

'Not your smile,' Jay told him. 'That smile is all your mother's—the wide and mischievous one I fell in love with when she was not much bigger than you are now.'

'If you loved her, then why did you leave her?' Kit demanded gruffly.

'Because I had to go to America, to work for a year,' Jay answered steadily. 'But, while I was away, your mother found out we were going to have you, so she wrote to me, telling me all about you and asking me to come back home to you both.' His eyes flicked briefly to Rebecca's still face then away again. 'Only I never received her letter. And consequently, when she got no reply from me, your mother thought I no longer cared for her, so she ran away. I don't blame her; she must have been very hurt and very angry. And you must not blame her either, Kit,' his father told him gravely. 'It had to have been the most frightening time for her, and yet she managed to look after you herself, has loved and cared for you, and made you into the kind of young man any father would be proud to have.'

So, it was to be told that way, was it? Rebecca sat staring down at her fingers where they played gently with her son's, and accepted drily that perhaps it was the only way—the cleaner way to tell it. At least Jay's version did not blacken anyone's character, and nor did it sully Kit's place in it all.

'But now we've all found each other again,' Jay went on solemnly after allowing the child a moment to take in everything he had said, 'and I would like to make it up to you both for the last ten years. Make us into the family we would have been if your mother's letter had not gone astray.'

'Where would we live?'

He was winning him over, Rebecca noted with an ache. Slowly, carefully, winning her son over.

'At my home, in Yorkshire,' Jay told him, Rebecca's look of mute protest glancing right off him. 'It will mean some big changes for all of us, but I think, if we all try our best, we could be very happy.'

When the boy did not instantly reject what he was telling him, Jay leaned forward in his seat in a way which centred the child's full attention on him, his gaze unswervingly concentrated on Kit's blue stare.

'I have a big house, Kit,' he went on huskily, 'set out in the Yorkshire countryside with its own wood, and lake, and private stretch of the river where your mother——'

'Does it have fish in it?' Kit asked eagerly, and Rebecca watched, hollow-hearted, as her son shifted his tense little frame closer to the edge of his own seat, being drawn unconsciously closer and closer to Jay.

Jay nodded and smiled. 'Enough fish for you to fish in there your whole life without catching the same one twice,' he said temptingly. 'Why, do you like fishing?'

'Oh, yes!' the boy replied, his blue eyes shining. 'Uncle Tom takes me—he's a teacher, you know,' he paused to explain, 'so he takes me in the school holidays when he can.'

'Well, when you come to live with me——' not 'if' Rebecca made rueful note, but 'when' . . . the child was really being given no choice though he didn't realise it '—you can go fishing whenever you wish, so long as your school homework is out of the way——'

'I'll have to go to a new school?' At last Jay had inadvertently hit on something Kit did not like, a frown darkening his blue eyes.

'Yes, of course,' his father replied calmly, 'but it will be the same village school your mother went to, small and friendly where everyone knows everyone else.'

'Did you go to that school?'

'No.' A cloud darkened Jay's face for a moment, the shadows of a man remembering the lonely life of a young boy sent away to boarding-school from too early an age, and Rebecca's heart squeezed despite itself, remembering that boy with him: the one who had had few friends in his home village, set apart by his exclusive rearing. A boy who had turned to a harum-scarum little girl for company because he'd had little other choice.

'I keep horses, too. . .' he went on briskly, then smiled and said ruefully, 'You should see your mother sitting astride a horse, Kit.' His blue eyes gleamed suddenly, that old wicked charm leaping out from behind the clouds to stir both child and mother. 'She rides like the wind itself, courageous and free; I don't think she was ever happier than when she was let gallop across the fields on Salamander's big powerful back——'

'Salamander?' Kit repeated while tears split Rebecca's vision. 'But that's the name of Mum's special dress label!'

'Yes, isn't it?' Jay glanced up to catch her look of pained reproach for what he was doing. I hate you for this! she told him silently. But he just flicked his attention back to Kit, ignoring her. 'Have you ever ridden a horse, Kit?' he asked quietly. The dark head shook, eyes wide and fixed unblinkingly on him. 'Would you like to learn how?' The dark head nodded, and Rebecca got up jerkily, unable to sit there and listen to any more, feeling the bleak cold shadow of defeat wash over her.

'Ex-excuse me,' she murmured huskily, 'I have to...' and walked quickly from the room before the tears aching to be let go burst despairingly from her.

CHAPTER TEN

'Won over, Chrissy,' Rebecca chokingly concluded the tale of her three-day-long nightmare, 'by private fishing rights and the chance to ride a horse!'

'Poor Becky,' Christina murmured in sympathy, having listened to it all come pouring out over a cup of coffee, while the firm worked happily beneath them without either of its owners in attendance.

'I can't believe it's all really happening to me!' Rebecca sighed out wretchedly. Jay was out—with his son. Gone joy-riding to win Kit's approval of his big fast car! God! She shuddered, recognising her own bitterness for what it was—jealousy, hard, hot, and burning jealousy. 'I can't compete with what Jay can offer Kit, and he knows it!'

'It has to have been hard for him,' Christina pointed out, already half won-over by Jay's easy charm, 'to find out after ten years that he has a son.'

'Hard for him to accept that son is alive, you mean,' she jeered, then grimaced at this next show of bitterness, but this time it came from another dark place inside her, a place which belonged to those first black months after she had fled from Thornley. 'I can't just dismiss the fact that he disowned all responsibility for Kit even before he was born.'

'No, I don't suppose you can,' her friend agreed. 'But—are you sure that letter actually got posted, love?' she questioned frowningly. 'I mean, this Olivia person sounds a real bitch to me. Maybe she didn't post the letter—maybe she——'

'She posted it,' Rebecca stated certainly, seeing again, as clearly as if it had happened only yesterday, Olivia

127

climbing out of her car and into the pouring rain to post that distinctive blue envelope in the post-box. She could still see her quick wave, her flashing white-toothed smile before she climbed back into her car and drove away again. 'She posted it,' she repeated. 'And Jay is the only person who could have fed his father the information he faced me with a week later.'

'The old tyrant,' Chrissy grunted. 'I can't believe that kind of outmoded snobbishness still goes on! God, it makes you want to kick something, doesn't it?'

With a sigh Rebecca got up, collecting their mugs and pushing them into the sink, then went still, staring bleakly out on to the rear view of the garden, her thoughts turning heavier by the minute.

'He expects us to go and live in Yorkshire,' she mumbled. 'Just up and leave everything we have here, as if the last ten years of *our* lives don't even matter!'

'Perhaps he's right, Rebecca, and they don't matter,' Christina argued gently. 'Life has a lousy way of making us face up to our mistakes. Jay is being made to face up to his in the heart-wrenching sight of his own son, grown to be nearly ten years old without his even being aware of his existence. Now you're being made to face up to all those things you ran away from ten years ago. Absolution for your sins lies in Yorkshire, Becky,' she murmured wisely. 'For everyone's sins: yours, Jay's and your mother's. And,' she went in a more positive tone, 'there would be no great hardship placed on the business by your living in Yorkshire instead of here. You've been saying yourself recently that it's becoming too much for you to work on Salamander as well as run things here— and live on top of it all too! Salamander designs are the ones which take up your personal time these days, while we all work on the run-of-the-mill stuff.'

'Salamander, Chrissy,' Rebecca reminded her sardonically, 'is what keeps the prices for the run of the mill stuff at the reasonable level our kind of customer can afford.'

'I'm not disputing that,' Christina said. 'And there is no reason why Salamander can't go on doing that—but with you working on the designs in Yorkshire while I work on the simpler, cheaper versions down here. After all, lovey,' she added drily, 'you and me both know that what the rich fools pay for a Salamander they can get under the Becky label for less than a tenth of the price! Just think about it, Becky,' she urged, 'safely tucked away in Yorkshire, you can give your whole attention to Salamander without all of—this...' she waved a hand which encompassed all the busy foray which went on day in day out beneath her '...getting in your way! It could, if you treated it all positively enough, just be the makings of the business! You would have time to create more Salamanders,' she went on eagerly, the idea growing on her more and more with every word she spoke. 'I'm sure Jay would let you convert one room in his home as a working studio for you—after all,' she added wryly, 'you did say the place was big enough to get lost in if you wanted to! Then, with this part of the house empty, we could begin utilising the space up here, bring in more machinery and more sewers, begin the crèche you've always wanted to have! Expand this side of the business, as we've known for some time it has been straining at the leash to do itself, only we've had to turn orders away because we're stretched to our furthest limits already!'

'My God,' Rebecca drawled, turning to stare at Christina's eager face. 'You have got it all worked out, haven't you?' Christina stared back at her, that deriding tone bringing a dark flush of colour running up her cheeks. Then tears split Rebecca's vision and she turned quickly away again. 'I'm sorry,' she whispered in shame. 'I really didn't mean that. It's just that...' She lifted a hand to her face, the fingers cold and trembling, her eyes hot with the tired sting of tears. 'Oh, God, Chrissy,' she choked out huskily. 'It's not the business I'm worried about. It's Jay, and how he intends taking his so-called revenge on me.'

Then the rigid hold she had been keeping on her emotions all day snapped, and the tears began to fall in earnest, wrenching her slender frame and sending her face fully into her trembling hands. Through the strains of her own wretchedness she heard Christina's chair scrape on the floor as she got up, then two hands came gently down on her shuddering shoulders at the same time as the kitchen door closed quietly behind someone. And, before she had a chance to realise it, she was being turned around and gathered into Jay's arms.

'Kit...' she murmured thickly, trying to pull away from him.

'Outside,' he said, not allowing her to move away, 'playing with a small boy whose mother is busy at work on one of your clever designs. You've got quite a little empire for yourself down there, haven't you, Rebecca?' he commended ruefully. 'Who'd have thought it of the wild and undisciplined gypsy I used to know?'

'I've worked hard for what I have, Jay,' she told him stiffly, struggling to bring the tears under control. 'Everything I have is rooted right here!' She fumbled between his hugging arms to wrest her hankie out of her trouser pocket, pushing it up between their bodies to dab her eyes. 'My home, my work, the self-respect I've worked so damned hard to earn!'

'And I suppose you think I mean to take all those things away from you?' he concluded, the deep bass tones of his voice resonant against her resting brow.

'You want revenge.'

'I want, Rebecca,' he told her sombrely, 'that which should never have been taken away from me in the first place.' He shifted, lifting his hand to grip her chin, forcing her to look into his hard handsome face to see the grim sincerity written there. 'Revenge is for the bitter, and I am not bitter, just—angry,' he sighed. 'Angry that so much has been lost to me because of the unfortunate misdirection of one important letter.'

She stiffened in his arms, impatient at his continual denial of any knowledge of that letter.

'You still don't believe me, do you?' he said through gritted teeth, recognising her withdrawal for what it was. 'Well, I don't know what I can do to prove it to you, Rebecca!' he said impatiently. 'Because it puts me in an impossible catch-twenty-two situation! If I could produce the letter it would prove I damned well received it! But insisting I never had it in the first place does not prove me innocent!'

'Oh, for God's sake!' she sighed, sick of the letter, sick of the past and what it had done to them all. 'I know you got the letter, dammit, because your own father told me so!'

He stared at her, his eyes gone silver with shock. 'What?' he breathed, seeming barely able to enunciate the word.

'You heard,' she said wearily, holding his blank stare with a derisive one of her own. 'I don't know how you expected your father to deal with it when you rang him to tell him about my letter,' she went on bitterly, 'but at least have the satisfaction of knowing he did it to his usual ruthless precision!'

He flinched—she watched it happen as her angry words plunged cuttingly into him. Then he was turning away from her, stumbling, like a man who had just lost the use of his legs, into a chair at her kitchen table, falling down in it to sit limp-limbed and drained.

'My father gave you money to get rid of our child,' he whispered hoarsely, 'didn't he?'

'You know he did, Jay,' she answered heavily. 'So why are you trying to look so surprised?'

'Tell me,' he demanded, not looking at her, but at some invisible point way back in his mind. 'Tell me from the very beginning what happened. I want to know.'

Rebecca gave a derisive smile. 'You already know most of it,' she said, not really wanting to go over what had been for her the worst time of her life. 'I wrote to you. You received my letter. Rang your father to ask him to deal with the problem of Rebecca Shaw for you, and he did, as I just said, with his usual acute precision!'

'All of it, dammit!' he barked out, making her blink, his eyes flashing a look of stark bitterness at her. 'Not just that...sarcastic little potted version you've just offered. I want to hear it all! All of it, dammit—all—*all*!'

She was so taken aback by the shuddering depth of emotion in his voice that it almost, *almost* convinced her that he had just received the most soul-destroying shock of his life! Then she dismissed the idea as weak. He was looking like that because he knew the truth was about to hit him squarely in the face at last. And that was what he couldn't cope with.

Quietly, with her own voice lost in the strained thickness of her throat, Rebecca did as he asked, beginning with his father's calling her up to the house, and not stopping until she reached the point where she'd boarded the train to leave Yorkshire for London with her blood money tucked safely away in her pocket and her solemn vow never to lay eyes on any of them again!

'Now are you going to deny all knowledge of my letter?' she taunted bitterly, feeling drained to the very dregs of her own miserable soul after that.

He didn't answer for a moment, and the silence had a dull, flat, empty feel to it as he sat there, staring at the ground, his body slack in the straight-backed kitchen chair as though someone had just effectively punched the life out of him. And Rebecca waited, arms folded, defences up high, for him to finish what really should never have begun.

'No,' he sighed at last. 'I don't suppose I am. Not after that.' He turned his head away from her, his fingers trembling slightly as he lifted them to squeeze the pressure-points either side of his long straight nose.

Outside, beyond the kitchen window, she could hear the light sound of Kit's playful voice interspersed with other childish cries. And beneath her feet she could feel the muted vibration of electric motors turning steadily, and felt nothing—nothing going on inside herself. It was as if time itself had just stopped, right here in this small neat room.

He lifted his head suddenly, and she saw the same ravaged expression she had seen on his face when he had first heard about Kit.

'They told me you ran away to abort Joe Tyndell's child,' he said gruffly.

Rebecca's head shot up, appalled horror darkening the grey of her eyes. 'But I told you differently!' she cried. 'In that letter you've tried so damned hard to deny all knowledge of!'

She shook her head, her soft mouth pursing in mute refusal to speak another single word on the subject. She would not demean herself by being forced into defending what she already knew to be the truth, and more to the point—what Jay knew to be the truth! And if he could have been so easily convinced that she would walk right out of his arms and into Joe Tyndell's like that then there was nothing left for them to say to each other!

'So, what do you want to do now?' he asked.

She stared at him in puzzled surprise. *He* was asking *her*? She'd thought it had all been decided already—by him. As far as she was concerned, what had just been said made no difference whatsoever to anything, except she had at last forced him to admit to her damned letter.

'You tell me,' she therefore drawled. 'You're the one with all the answers.'

'Yes,' he breathed, and a strange expression touched his mouth, hard and bleak and self-derogatory. 'I am, aren't I?' Yet the silence fell again, stretching out like piano wire between them while he just continued to sit there, offering nothing. Nothing at all.

'Look...' she sighed, weary of it all—wearied to death of it all, 'I'll make you a bargain, Jay.' She levelled her cool grey eyes on his. 'It's obvious, even to me, that, now you've firmly established yourself as Kit's father, I can't do anything about it without having to hurt him to do it. So,' she took in a deep breath and let it out again, 'I'll agree to the marriage thing you dropped so damned arrogantly on my lap this morning. I shall even pretend—for my son's sake and perhaps for our own pride's sake,' she added cynically, 'to be madly and blindly in love with you again if that's what you want! But,' she went on coldly, staring at his lean handsome profile with eyes washed as clear and bleak as the winter day beyond the kitchen window '...only on condition that you don't bring the past up again, because our only hope in making a good and healthy environment for Kit to grow up in is if we can both forget the damned past, and what it did to all our lives!'

He didn't answer straight away, seeming to be struggling not to lose himself back in the dark tracks of his mind. Then he smiled, a bleak and rueful kind of little smile, and got up, his limbs still slack and uncoordinated, though he pulled himself up to his full impressive height before saying drily, 'Well, I suppose you can't be fairer than that under the circumstances.' Then he turned his dark head, the bleakness more evident in his gaze as he looked at her. 'You always were a fair-minded little thing, weren't you, Becky? Loyal and true to those you loved.' A look entered his eyes, disturbing with its depth of cynicism which seemed to be aimed entirely inwards. 'You don't really owe any of us a single thing, do you?'

'I owe Kit,' she said. 'And if he wants you he can have you.'

He lowered his dark head and shook it slowly, as if he was having difficulty understanding it all, then smiled again, and the first quiver of apprehension began filtering through her as he smoothly closed the small gap separating them.

'Ah,' he murmured softly, sending her arching back against the kitchen sink in an effort to get away from the gentle finger he brought up to draw in a light taunt down her cheek, 'but does little Becky want me? I find myself wondering,' he posed curiously. 'And if she does...' the finger came to rest at the quivering corner of her mouth '...then I have then to ask myself, Why? *Why?* After everything I've damned well done to her!'

'Jay?' she gasped in sudden alarm, but, even as she said it, he closed the gap between their mouths.

It spread like molten fire through her, the instant, stinging grip of desire holding her in its dizzying thrall as he swung her away on a kiss which broke all previous bounds by its sheer lack of sexual provocation. He touched her nowhere else, just his lips moving warmly on hers, lighting senses she did not want lit, sending that hated track trickling through her veins until they broke apart, both gasping for breath, and Jay looked down the full length of her where her hands lay tightly clenched at her sides and her breasts pulsed with the pounding thump of her agitated heart.

'Yes...' he whispered triumphantly. 'She wants me.'

'No.' The denial fell from hot and trembling lips, and he smiled at it, taunting it, treating it with the contempt it deserved.

'Yes...' he said again. 'It's called sex, Rebecca,' he told her, drawing the evocative word out like a promise, 'that delicious, clamouring meeting of the senses which has you crying out in my arms and that,' he then added grimly, 'I suppose, will have to do for now...'

Then, before she could question what he meant, he had covered her mouth again. The world went into a spin, her senses whipping out to wrap themselves tightly around him, not even giving her the small satisfaction of a short moment's struggle before she was bending into his desire like a slender reed to a raging wind. She could feel every single nuance of the man like a billion pricks of awareness on her hot and sensitised flesh. He moulded her, thigh to thigh, hip to grinding, sensual hip, breast to throbbing, pulsing breast. And their mouths strained against each other, tongues locked and battling, the breath mingling in the hot and frenzied explosion of desire.

Unexpectedly, he pushed her away from him, holding her at arm's length to view and exalt in the ravages he had wrought on her icy composure. 'And whatever happened ten years ago, Becky, none of it—nothing—nothing has managed to change this, has it?' he challenged harshly. 'You still want me so badly that you tremble with it when I so much as touch you! And, God help me—I still want you in the same damned crucifying way!'

He found her mouth again, and she let him take it, exalting in the violence of the kiss, conceding everything, which was what he wanted her to do, proving to them both just who reigned supreme, no matter what had gone on in the past.

They were so engrossed in each other that they didn't hear the clatter of small feet on the stairs, or even the quick opening of the kitchen door. It was Kit's gasped, 'Oh!' which awoke them to their shocked audience, but Jay stopped her from pulling away from him, holding her trapped intimately against his body while he turned to glance at his mortified son.

'Have you never seen your mother being thoroughly kissed before?' he teased Kit gently.

'No,' Kit mumbled, so red in the face with embarrassment that he glowed with it.

'Then get used to it, son,' Jay told him, turning back to gaze at Rebecca with dark and dusky challenge, 'because you will be seeing your mother and me kissing a lot from now on.'

Staking—staking his rights in every way he could do, Rebecca thought wearily to herself when, at last, Jay gave her a bit of respite from his brutal domination over every part of both her and Kit's life—by commandeering her small office to use as his own so he could turn that bludgeoning mind of his on the poor whipped souls who worked for him, via the telephone.

Kit was watching television in the other room, his mood difficult to decipher because he had taken his feelings underground, avoiding even looking at her while he tried to come to terms with the shattering events which had overtaken his young life today.

Rebecca sighed to herself, turning her face up to the window in front of her to gaze out on the bleak half-light of the afternoon, her fingers stilling on the mundane job of peeling potatoes for the tea she was supposed to be preparing.

What was she letting herself in for, she wondered, by allowing Jay to railroad her into doing everything his way? *Was* it a railroading, though? a small derisive little voice asked inside her head. Or are you only conceding everything to him because he's only demanding of you what you actually want yourself?

Kit, she told herself firmly, glancing back at the half-peeled potato lying in her palm. You're doing it for Kit.

But that little voice laughed, and the derision was harder this time to ignore.

She had loved Jay as completely at sixteen as anyone could have loved another human being. Her youth hadn't mattered, or her lack of worldly experience, because that love had been maturing steadily through years of knowing and being with him. What had happened when he'd gone away had broken her in two, because his defection had left her with nothing—not a single thing to hang on to—and, like any badly injured animal, she had gone crawling away to lick her wounds, surviving only by pure instinct, fighting back with the only weapons he had left her with—her pain and her anger to keep her going, running, hiding—and, she at last admitted to herself, paying him back in her own way by never making contact, never giving him a single chance to see the damage he had done to her. And each time she had looked at her son as a small babe in arms, as a bright and enchanting toddler, and as a young man growing through his years with the same grace and pride his father possessed in greater quantity, she knew she had been looking Jay in the eye and saying, 'See! This is mine! He loves me! He is a part of you you will never take away from me!'

Now Jay was challenging even that, wanting her son for his own, the son she had borne and loved and nurtured, cried over, hurt with and for. And as payment he was willing to take her back into his arms, feed her with those terrible weakening feelings of love and passion which had always kept her faithful to him, even through the last ten dark years.

She shivered, seeing the next ten years becoming no lighter, no less difficult to bear because this time...this time she could not even kid herself that Jay loved her. So she would let him take her body, wreak his earth-moving magic over her, and have to live with the fact that she gave herself for no other reason than to ease this terrible need she had for him.

You love, that intrusive little voice reminded her. You love—can't that be enough for you? But that love had lost its respect, and without it she felt nothing better than the tramp his father had accused her of being, living with a man for the gratification he could offer her between the sheets at night, loving him, but in a hard bitter way. Not love at all really, but the flip side of love, blighted, grudging. The darker side of desiring.

'Is there anything to drink?' a muted voice asked behind her, and she turned to find Kit standing awkwardly in the kitchen doorway, his expression guarded and sullen.

'Sure,' she said lightly, feeling another notch twist itself into her already tangled emotions. If Kit was already on his guard with her what kind of relationship did they have to look forward to in the future? 'Orange—or blackcurrant?' She went over to the fridge and opened the door, waiting for him to make up his mind.

'Orange, please.' He came to stand beside her as she poured a quantity of the cordial into a glass then took it to the sink to dilute it with cold water.

'Are you—OK, Kit?' she asked him quietly, levelling him with one of her warm, solemn stares.

He shrugged, turning his face away. 'I suppose,' he answered vaguely.

'If you have any—objections to my and your father's plans, then you must speak out and tell us, you know.' She handed him the glass, and watched him stare grimly at the orange liquid without trying to taste it. 'Neither of us, not your father or I, want to do anything which will make you unhappy.' She stroked a gentle hand across his silk-smooth hair, and, unable to resist it, murmured huskily, 'I love you, darling.'

His eyes shot up to clash with hers. 'More than you love him?'

So that was it! Relieved that that was all it was, she took the glass from his hand and put it aside so she could go down on her knees and gather him in.

'I love you more than I love anyone else in this world, Kit,' she told him softly. 'And that's the honest truth of it.'

'It hurts me inside when I see him with you.' Her throat began to work in response to that pained little confession, and she held him closer, a sudden movement at the door bringing her pained eyes upwards to find Jay standing there, perfectly still, listening. 'He says he wants me, but really it's you he wants, isn't it? I don't really count at all!'

'Oh, no darling!' Horrified that he could be thinking such a crazy thing, Rebecca drew him out to arm's length, ignoring Jay so she could hold her son's hurting gaze with the fierce blaze of her own. 'Your father loves you! Of course he does!' she insisted positively.

'I don't want him to take you away from me!' the poor child sobbed out shakily. 'I l-like him,' he admitted, 'but I l-love you more! W-what if I don't like it in Y-Yorkshire? W-what if I want to come back here? He m-might not let you come with me, and then what will I do?'

'Oh, Kit . . .' Rebecca pulled him into the hugging warmth of her arms, thinking heavily that poor Kit probably had it the wrong way around and that if anyone would be wanting to come back here it would be herself.

'I just don't want to share you with him, Mum,' Kit admitted into her warm throat.

'The sharing works all ways, Kit,' she told him gravely, seeing Jay's bitter grimace at the child's plaintive thrust. 'I shall have to get used to sharing you with him, too. Just as he will have to get used to sharing with both of us. Love is like that, darling,' she murmured against his warm, damp cheek. 'Being a family means loving and sharing everything, but it doesn't mean that we each get less of that love, only that our love swells like a big bubble to accommodate everyone in it.'

'And what if I can't learn to love him?'

Jay flinched, and Rebecca found she had it in her to feel for him, truly feel for him at last. 'I shall be very surprised if you don't.' She smiled, seeing herself at Kit's age, her grey eyes glowing with devotion for Jay, her hero. 'But no one is expecting instant devotion from you, Kit,' she went on more seriously, pushing the child at arm's length so she could look him gravely in the eye. 'You are going to have to learn to know your father, just as he is going to have to learn to know you. And I think both of you must give yourselves time for that, don't you?'

He nodded gravely, his blue eyes hooded now because he was beginning to regret his momentary outburst. 'Just so long as he knows that you're mine too,' he mumbled, then more assertively, 'You will tell him that, won't you?'

'Yes.' She lifted her eyes back to the door, but Jay was no longer there. He had slipped away again as silently as he had come, and as she turned her gaze back to Kit she heard the quiet click of her bedroom door closing behind him. 'I'll tell him,' she promised, knowing she did not have to tell Jay anything. He had overheard every plaintive word.

CHAPTER ELEVEN

'MARRIED!' Lina Shaw lay against her bank of pillows, her sallow face glowing with a new light which was in itself almost enough to make it all worthwhile to Rebecca. 'Oh, this has to be the best thing that could have happened for you all!'

Her grey eyes did a shining scan of all three of them, Jay standing big and real beside Rebecca, his arm a possessive clamp around her waist, and Kit sitting on the bed beside her, suffering his grandmother's wondering touches and tearful smiles because he knew she was poorly and must be humoured.

'It makes everything right again, doesn't it?' she sighed contentedly. 'Puts the past where it belongs: in the past. Oh, you can't know how much it means to me to be able to do that.'

'Perhaps we do, Lina, since we feel exactly the same way,' Jay agreed for both of them, smiling through the touch of cynicism Rebecca caught in his voice.

He didn't believe that any more than she did. Any more than she had when she had insisted on just that point herself. No more talk of the past and I shall adhere to everything you want, she'd said. But in reality the past still stood between them, colouring every guarded word they said to each other, sending them tiptoeing around subjects which could ignite an explosion, watching, waiting for—she knew not what, she acknowledged on an inner sigh, knowing only that a wary kind of truce lay between them, cool and unnaturally calm, like the eye of a storm before the real fury began.

They had been married that same morning, just before they made the long trip back up here—another of his immovable plans.

'We go home a united front,' he'd insisted when she had protested at the frankly terrifying speed with which he was taking them over. 'You know of old what small country village life is like, Rebecca. All malicious gossip and wild exaggeration. If we issue them with a *fait accompli*, the dirt-digging and accompanying dust will settle a whole lot sooner.'

'The dirt being mine, I must assume,' she'd murmured acidly.

Jay had looked at her through cool, implacable eyes. 'The dirt belonging to *both* of us, since it is obvious to anyone who looks at Kit that he has to be my son. And it's him I am trying to protect,' he'd pointed out grimly. 'I don't want any of the muck-raking to reach his vulnerable ears. So to marry right away means they can have several weeks to get it all out of the way before I let him loose near them. I mean to take the next six weeks off work to get to know him, Rebecca,' he had informed her determinedly. 'After overhearing that little talk between you and him this afternoon, I decided it was the best and perhaps the only way to plant some solid roots for a future relationship. Kit can take lessons at the Hall from me for the rest of this term, then begin school in the village after the Easter break. That way I can be constantly around to guard him from any vicious tongues, and be with him for long enough stretches for us to learn more about each other.'

'And Olivia?' she had thrown tartly at him, remembering how much he had enjoyed telling her how Olivia was such an intimate part of his life.

'She will have to accept it along with everyone else,' he'd said coolly. 'She has no special claims on me, after all.'

'Not even as a lover?' she'd clipped, angered by his cold, dismissive tone. 'Or are you intending having your cake and eating it too, Jay, by keeping her dangling until you've tired yourself of me again?'

'I don't envisage it being any hardship remaining faithful to you, Rebecca,' he'd told her quietly, then, after studying her bitterly cynical face for a long moment, had pulled her resisting body into his arms to add sardonically, 'so long as you keep enthralling my nights as passionately as you have been doing!'

He'd closed the subject then by making love to her until she'd begged for mercy.

'You should have had a honeymoon...'

Rebecca blinked, flushing a little when she realised just where her thoughts had gone off to.

'All newly-weds should have a few weeks to themselves to get to know each other properly,' her mother was saying scoldingly.

Rebecca allowed herself a wry smile at that, because there was no way she and Jay could know each other any more intimately than they did now. During the week they had spent in London making arrangements for the small wedding, organising the special licence, seeing to the necessary problems splitting her business in two inevitably caused, Jay had made sure they'd learned about each other in the frenzied darkness of the nights, when he'd devoured her with his body, piling sensual pressure upon sensual pressure in his effort to make her every thought and feeling as his own.

'But we are...' she heard Jay say now, and once again had to force herself to concentrate as the hand on her waist moved upwards until his fingers lay just beneath the steady beat of her heart. Instantly the beat quickened, the warm brush of his fingers against the underside of her breast sending a stinging sensation of heat rippling through her. 'I've taken six weeks off work to be with Kit and Rebecca—surely that's honeymoon enough for anyone.' Shrewdly, he made sure Kit knew he was considered a part of this 'honeymoon' he was talking about. 'And perhaps, by the end of that, you'll be thinking of coming back home to us so that you can join in the fun too!' He grinned, warming Rebecca's reluctant heart at this thoughtfulness in including her mother.

But her mother's face clouded over, her thoughts going off somewhere dark inside herself. 'I don't think so, Jay,' she murmured emptily. 'I don't think your father would approve, and I certainly don't think I can bring myself to impose on you all—not after what I——'

'Kit,' Rebecca put in sharply, staying her mother's tongue before she said something in front of her grandson they would all regret. He glanced round questioningly. 'Why don't you take the lift down to the ground floor and see if the drinks vending-machine is working down there?' she suggested.

Glad of the excuse to escape, he scrambled down from the bed. 'I'll take him,' Jay offered, sensitively recognising that mother and daughter still had a lot to say to each other before their relationship could begin to settle into something worthwhile, and he held out his hand to Kit, who took it shyly, and led the boy out of the room. The old lady lay red-cheeked, aware that her daughter had just issued what came as close as it could do to a reprimand to her mother.

'I'm sorry,' she whispered as soon as they were alone. 'That was rather foolish of me, but . . .'

Rebecca sighed a little as she moved to take Kit's place on the bed. Immediately her mother clutched at her hands.

'It's just that I still find my own part in it all too much to bear—especially after seeing him, Becky,' she choked. 'To think I actually wanted you to——!'

'Now stop that!' Rebecca said firmly, afraid her mother was going to agitate herself into another seizure. 'I won't listen to it, do you hear? We all have our guilts to bear, Mother,' she went on less harshly, 'but Jay and I have decided to make this a new beginning for all of us, and you'll only ruin that if you persist in making yourself ill over something which never actually happened!'

'But why didn't it happen?' Lina asked curiously. 'Why didn't you go through with it as we all thought you must have done?'

Kill Jay's child? she thought. Her smooth dark eyebrows rose in faint contempt. 'I never even contemplated it, to tell you the truth,' she said, then grimaced, recalling the way they'd all shouted around her, bullying her, stating their opinions at her until she'd thought she would scream if they didn't listen to her. But they never had. Not Jay's father or her own mother.

'He told me it was Joe Tyndell's child, you know.'

'Who did?' Rebecca asked sharply, going cold inside at the thought that Jay could have said such a cruel thing to her mother.

'Jay's father. When he called me into his study. He told me you were lying and it was not Jay's baby. He said he would have it known all over the village that you were trying to foist another man's child on his son. He said that either you and the child went, or we all went and he would make sure nobody else ever employed me in a place of trust again!' Her shoulders began to shake with the weight of it all, the need to get it off her chest a grim fact Rebecca accepted at last. 'And—weak, weak fool that I was, I let myself believe him. And I was frightened.' Her gnarled hands tore wretchedly at Rebecca's. 'I was so afraid for myself that I didn't give a single thought to how frightened and alone you must have been feeling! N-not until you'd gone, and I began to think more clearly, and then it was too late, wasn't it?' The old eyes looked grim as they sought Rebecca's. 'But the worst of it all, Becky,' she whispered guiltily, 'is that I knew all along that if you were having a baby then it had to be Jay's. I may have been a poor mother to you, dear, but I had eyes in my head. I knew you and Jay were in love. I could see it in his face every time he looked at you, see it in the way you bloomed for him that summer, looking as though you only had to reach for the moon to touch it because Jay had already given it to you!' She sighed, sinking tiredly back against the pillows, her face, though not quite so twisted as it had been, still pale and drawn. 'And, unlike you, I think,' she went on candidly, 'I could see the advantages Jay's love would bring your way. So, even though I disapproved of the intimacy of your relationship, I said nothing, and let it go on, imagining you living at the big house one day, Jay's wife, and mistress of that beautiful home I had cared for for so long!' A long sigh shook her, bleak and full of shame. 'If anyone was guilty of bad thoughts then it was me, Rebecca, not you. You just loved, loved from the heart, while I watched and waited, feeling rather pleased with events. I knew Jay's father was lying,' she murmured huskily. 'I knew there was no way on this earth his interpretation could be true. But, when it came to a show-down I saved my own neck at the expense of yours. And that, Becky, was my biggest sin of all.'

The drive home from the hospital was littered with curious questions from Kit, who was eager to learn all he could about his new surroundings. But, while Rebecca answered as brightly as she could, her thoughts were struggling to go inwards, lose herself in the bleak and lonely picture her mother had painted of her life during the last ten guilt-ridden years.

It had not been worth it; none of it. If only...

She shivered, stopping herself from sinking into a miserable bout of if onlys, because they served no purpose whatsoever.

'OK?' Jay murmured, turning to glance at her.

She nodded her head, and he smiled, reaching out to pick up one of her hands and move it over to rest on his hard-muscled thigh, keeping it there with the warm cover of his own. 'She's going to be all right, darling,' he said quietly, accurately reading where her thoughts were fixed. 'Like all of us, it's going to take your mother time to come to terms with herself for what she did, but eventually we all forget—forgive ourselves, even.'

Something in the sudden bleak light in his eyes told
Rebecca that he was talking as much about himself as
he was her mother. 'And we have Kit,' he went on briskly,
'the best panacea of all!' He gave a gentle squeeze of
her resting hand before removing his so that he could
slow the car down through the gears. 'Hey, Kit!' he
commanded his son's attention. 'Look to your left, son,
and you'll see your new home come into view.'

'Golly...' Rebecca heard her son murmur in breathless
awe. 'Are we going to be living in—that?'

'That' had a few surprises waiting for both mother
and son when they got inside—one of them being the
completely refurbished rooms Jay had ordered to be
made ready for Kit just a few doors further along the
wing from the master suite his parents were going to be
sharing from now on, and, if Kit had been slightly over-
awed by the size and grandeur of his new home, then,
as Jay showed them the large suite which was to be Kit's
own from now on, the child just stood staring around
him as though he couldn't believe what his eyes were
telling him!

'How did you manage this?' Rebecca murmured
huskily, touched, unbearably touched by this inspired
piece of thoughtfulness as she, like Kit, gazed around
the comfy sitting-room with its familiar pale green
velveteen three-piece suite and cheap but serviceable
furniture—everything in fact, from their London sitting-
room, rearranged here for Kit's personal use. Even his
own single bed was here, waiting for him in the bedroom,
complete with his old Batman duvet cover.

'Everything was packed and brought up by road this
morning, just after we left,' Jay told her. 'I...' he looked
down at his feet, for a moment appearing oddly awkward
'...I remember what it was like being nine and having
to sleep in a strange bed in a strange place. I didn't want
Kit to know the—emptiness that can fill you with.'

Her heart squeezed when she recalled how Jay had
told her about that frightening and lonely time in his

life when he had been shipped off to boarding-school with nothing—nothing familiar around him he could glean any hint of comfort from.

'Well, thank you.' She reached out to touch his arm, and their eyes met, a wave of that old warmth and understanding they once shared passing between them.

'Hey—Mum!' Kit broke the powerful moment, making her dark lashes flicker as she forced her attention away from Jay and on to Kit. 'I've even got our old telly!' He grinned, then looked uncertainly at his father. 'This stuff doesn't really go with this house, does it?' he mumbled perceptively.

Jay smiled, walking further into the room to go and ruffle the top of his son's dark head. 'Never judge a book by its cover,' he advised. 'It's what goes on inside it which really counts.'

Kit frowned at him in puzzlement, not understanding the cryptic remark, but Rebecca understood, and knew he wasn't talking about furniture.

'The point is, Kit,' Jay went on in a more natural tone, 'I thought it might help you feel more at home here to have the things you're used to having around you. And, as far as anyone else in the house is concerned, these are your own private rooms, where you can come and be comfortable whenever you like without having to worry about putting your feet up on the furniture or marking some damned priceless antique or other...'

Another refrain from the past, Rebecca recognised, and once again her heart moved in sympathy for that younger Jay—fifteen years old and growing too quickly to have the grace and co-ordination his body possessed now—who had come looking for her, broodily kicking at stones, hands shoved morosely into his jeans pockets because he'd just received another rocket for accidentally knocking against some treasure or other, or simply been caught by his father with his shoes on inside the house. That boy would have given anything to have had a place like this where he could just go and slouch around with no one to scold him for his need for slovenliness then.

'Come on,' he strode back to Rebecca's side, taking her arm and leading her out of Kit's room, 'I've got what I hope is a pleasant surprise for you, too.'

Puzzled and faintly wary, Rebecca let him guide her back towards the stairs and then around the gracefully curving landing which took them into the other wing of the house. Several doors along he stopped and opened one, then stood back to allow her to precede him inside; she did so with some trepidation, wondering what was going to hit her, then went perfectly still, as awed in her own way as Kit had been when she found herself standing in the kind of room she had only ever dared dream of possessing.

'What do you think?' Jay asked after letting her explore the huge working studio he'd had set up for her personal use. Everything was there, carefully unpacked and waiting for her. Her huge cutting-table, her bolts of fine fabric set on shelves across one wall. Her sewing machines, dress-rails, and the old-fashioned wood filing cabinet which housed all her precious patterns.

'I think you've gone to a lot of trouble,' she said quietly.

He grimaced, as if her flat-toned reply had disappointed him. 'I want you to be happy here, Rebecca,' he then said huskily.

She didn't answer, because happiness was something she didn't expect to find at Thornley. Happiness came with love and trust, and she didn't dare allow herself to feel either.

That night he made love to her with a new kind of urgency, staking ownership over her body, even if he would never reach any other part of her again. And, as if he sensed that hard core of reticence in her, he drove her to the very edge of insanity with his loving, only to stop when deep inside her, anchoring himself to her with the quivering power of his thighs as he glared hotly down on her.

'One day I'll make you say those special three little words to me again, Rebecca!' he threatened rawly, his eyes dark with angry passion as they burned down into hers. 'They'll slide breathlessly from your lips at a moment like this when your senses take over from your cold hard bitterness, and that's when I'll know you're *all* mine again!'

'I love you, Jay!' she mocked him with that old impassioned voice of her reckless youth, then stared at him through bright taunting eyes. 'Is that what you long to hear?' she asked him, utterly deriding their sincerity.

'You cruel little bitch!' he choked, and drove into her hard, his violent aggression matched all the way by her own.

It set a pattern for their future relationship. Jay had announced his grim intention to make her fall in love with him all over again, and she had challenged it with the deriding scorn of her voice.

It was over two weeks later, when they were coming back from the hospital one afternoon, that Rebecca saw a thoughtfully brooding look on Jay's face, and wondered ruefully what plans he was concocting now to make her sit up and take notice of him this time. Every time she saw that look these days it usually preceded one of his announcements gauged to get her back up, knock her off balance, or just downright confuse her. And the brooding look had been more intense than usual today, she realised uncomfortably, coming with him out of his study where he had spent the morning working at his desk, and staying with him throughout lunch and their visit to the hospital.

The look went along with a little game he was playing with all of them, with variations on the same theme depending on who he was playing it with. With her mother it was all charm and teasing; with Kit a clever blend of work and play.

Her mother had been moved out of the intensive care unit and into a ward with three other beds in it, all occupied by women of a similar age to herself, and, with Jay's special brand of charm, he soon had all four ladies eating out of his hand, and brought the light of laughter back into her mother's eyes, in his way encouraging her to put aside her brooding guilts.

Kit, on the other hand, was becoming more relaxed and content with his new life with every passing day. The big house had intimidated him at first, sending him creeping about as though he were an intruder, whispering instead of using the full clear tones of his usual chatty voice, jumping if anyone so much as spoke to him. Now he walked as arrogantly as his father through the elegant rooms, thought nothing of cuffing the suit of armour on his way past it, and enjoyed pulling ugly faces at his ancestors when he walked up the stairs. He was still a little wary of Jay, but only in as much as he was coming close to hero-worshipping him. Whatever Jay said Kit took grave and intense notice of. Whatever Jay did Kit watched with the kind of concentration which said he was fascinated with him, whether it was riding on the back of the mighty Salamander, or lazing slothfully in a comfortable chair after dinner.

Jay taught Kit his English and arithmetic, how to ride the shiny black pony he had purchased especially for him, and how to play chess. And Kit taught Jay how to feel the uplifting pleasure in just kicking a football around the low pasture by the lake, and how to play Chase the Ace. And, not by one flicker of his blue gaze, did Jay let his son know that it was he who had taught the mother who had then taught the son to play the card game in the first place!

And with her? Well, with her it was sex and—sex.

Since it was the only manner with which he managed to gain what he called a 'healthy' response from her,

that was where his efforts were all focused. In bed or
out of it, he used his sex appeal to keep her forever on
her nerve-ends, waiting for him to disturb her senses in
one way or another.

He played them all like perfectly tuned instruments in
his own orchestra of things, and what he got out of it
all Rebecca had no idea. Certainly, he seemed happy,
quite content to live out his life to the end of his days
in this detached kind of contentment he had adopted.

'I think we'll give a small party this weekend,' he murmured suddenly, not turning to look at her but keeping
his eyes fixed on the road ahead. 'Just to get the show
officially on the road, so to speak.'

So that was what all the brooding was about.
'Throwing us in at the deep end, are you, Jay?' she
mocked him drily.

Until now the Hall had discouraged visitors of any
kind, using the builders working on the renovation of
the Lodge to turn anyone away who might have decided
to chance their luck. Now, it seemed, just as she was
beginning to relax a little, all that nice comforting protection was going to stop.

'Not really, no,' he denied. 'I just think it better if we
don't hide ourselves away as though we have something
to be ashamed of. Just some close friends on—say—
Sunday afternoon for cocktails,' he decided. 'People with
children around Kit's age so he can get to know a few
of the local kids.'

'I thought you intended spending these weeks pro-
tecting him from all of that.'

'I decided it might be more constructive if we wean
him in slowly. That way, by the time he does start school,
he will have a few children he can relate to—ones who
will by then, hopefully, like him enough to shield him
from the other more—vocal ones. Joe Tyndell has a little
boy only a year or so younger than Kit. We could invite
him, I suppose...' he suggested thoughtfully.

'Joe Tyndell?' Rebecca stiffened, an icy suspicion shivering down her spine as she glanced sharply at his inscrutable profile. What was he up to now? she wondered nervously. Joe Tyndell was no friend of Jay's! They had been at each other's throats since as far back into her memory as she could go! 'Since when has Joe Tyndell been a welcome visitor to your home?' she asked him watchfully.

'*Our* home,' he corrected.

'Your home,' she stubbornly insisted. 'It still feels like a luxury hotel to me. A place where the decadent go to pamper their exclusive bodies.' Her expression was full of contempt.

Jay smiled at her, that forever-present insidious charm of his mocking her with a look. 'So you didn't like making love in the decadent luxury of my jacuzzi, did you?' he murmured silkily, the smile widening as her cheeks warmed. 'Some night that was last night, my sweet torment,' he drawled appreciatively, while she seethed hotly inside with her own sinking embarrassment. 'By the time we climbed out I'd got the strongest feeling you felt well and truly pampered, darling——'

'Shut up,' she said, wishing Kit were with them to protect her from his father's taunts, but he wasn't. Today he had stayed at home to help old Jimmy in the stables—a place she could hardly drag her son away from these days. 'Getting back to this party idea of yours,' she reverted quickly. 'What if I say I don't want to meet anyone just yet?'

Jay arched his brows at her. 'Then, my darling,' he told her lazily, 'I would just have to put myself out to—persuade you, wouldn't I?'

Her blood ran to fire at the husky implication he was making, and she had to turn her face away so he wouldn't see the effect his threat had on her turbulent eyes.

'*Sex...*' he whispered sensuously, just for the hell of seeing her stir restlessly in her seat, then laughed, and turned his attention back to the road.

Since that first time they had made love in her bed in London, over three weeks ago now, she couldn't get enough of him, and Jay knew it, playing on her weaknesses to the full, revelling in this one vital place where he had total control over her every thought and sense, using it to taunt her. He could make her burn with just a look. If she was speaking, make her stumble over her words by just running his lazy gaze down the front of her body.

If she was the controlled Mrs Jason Lorence in every other facet of their lives, where her senses were concerned she was a vampire, desperate to feed on the pleasures he could offer her body without any hope of controlling herself. And if she was ashamed of her own lack of self-command, then she gained some small comfort from knowing that she could affect him in exactly the same way—if she chose to, which she did not. And that, she had an idea, irritated him more than anything else in the war of nerves they were fighting—that she refused to tease him in any way, unless, of course, he had first reduced her to a mass of wanton witchery.

'Tonight I think we'll try it in the sauna,' he decided, doing it again, as always, prodding and poking at her before she could have a chance to rebuild her defences against him. 'Get all hot and sweaty,' he described with husky relish, 'then kind of—slide together. It should be quite——'

'Will you stop being so damned—crude?' she snapped, rising to his baiting, her pulses already hammering in response.

'That's not crude!' he denied, sending her an offended glance. 'It sounds damned well fantastic to me!'

CHAPTER TWELVE

AND Jason was right—it was fantastic. He had always been an exciting and imaginative lover, who, by his early tutelage, had brought out the same uninhibited desire for excellence in Rebecca. But that night surpassed all the other exquisite nights, with her body arching slickly on top of his while he held her above him, his mouth clinging to her breasts, the steam, the heat, and the sweet disturbing scent of their clean perspiration permeating all around them, the salacious hiss of moisture on hot coals, and the low husky sounds of their laboured breathing as they moved, slick, shining and steamy hot on each other, all culminating in the slowest, deepest, most sensual climax they had shared to date.

And afterwards, when he picked up her limp body in his arms and carried her, cradled closely to his heaving chest, into the shower, they kissed for the first time without the sex to colour their feelings. And Jay looked intently down at her, holding them both beneath the tepid spray, and forced her eyes to look deeply into his own and see, see what she had been refusing to see since she had walked reluctantly back into his life.

'I love you, Becky,' he confirmed with words what his eyes were telling her. 'I always have and I always will. Choose not to believe me if you will. But it will always be there, waiting for you. I love you, and there isn't a damned thing either you or I can do about it.'

And, funnily enough, she believed him. But what kind of man was he who could love like this and yet have so casually forsaken her when she had needed him the most?

Jay waited, watching the play of troubled emotions pass across her face, the intensity of his own regard almost begging her to reciprocate in kind, but Rebecca lowered her spiky lids over her eyes, unable, even though she loved him, to commit herself so completely to him again. She just didn't dare. Because if Jay ever betrayed her a second time she knew she would not survive the pain of it.

Would the pain be any less for not telling him? that niggling little voice in her head prodded ruthlessly. No, she answered it hollowly. But at least, this time, I would keep my pride.

The silence between them grew long and heavy, the only movement around them coming from the hissing spray from the shower-head, sending its cascade of water over his shoulders and down the long muscular length of him, splashing as it went on to her breasts, love-sore and swollen from his kisses, the dark nipples taut and erect, calling for him, as always calling for him.

As if he knew, he reached up to cup them in his palms, testing their weight as he had done all those years ago when they had come together that very first time. And tears pushed at the backs of her lids, a helpless yearning for what once had been crushing the muscles around her heart. He bent his head and licked her, and on her broken gasp straightened again, his eyes bleak and grim now, a light seeming to have gone out inside him.

'I love you,' he said again flatly. 'God knows how I'm going to deal with it if you can't bring yourself to love me again. But there it is; I love you,' and his mouth covered hers, warm and trembling on the power of his own pained emotion. Then he was shoving himself away from her and turning, his dark head averted, and without another word he left her alone, wilting miserably against the shower wall.

She had expected him to withdraw behind his shell after that, yet, strangely, he didn't. Even when she walked back into the bedroom half an hour later, her own expression guarded as she approached the bed where he lay staring emptily at the ceiling, the moment he saw her he smiled, and held out a hand in invitation for her to come to him.

That was the night she sobbed her heart out, brokenly and unexplainingly wept until there were no more tears left to weep, while he held her close, and said nothing, his hand gently smoothing down the long damp length of her hair until she fell, exhausted, into a deep, dreamless sleep.

The next day he brought up the subject of the party again by handing Rebecca a list of people he wanted to invite. Seeing Olivia's name right there at the top of the list stunned her, and any discomfort she might have been feeling for the way she had treated his declaration the night before disappeared on a surge of bitter jealousy. So Olivia was to remain a cosy part of his life, was she?

'Shouldn't you be the one to invite these people?' she snapped out tartly. 'After all, they're all your friends, not mine.'

'You're my wife now, aren't you?' he came back haughtily. 'You can see to it while I put Kit through his arithmetic,' he said, and walked arrogantly from the room, leaving her seething in silence behind him.

For the rest of that day—and the week—she avoided Jay like the plague. The invitations angrily written out and posted, she went to the bright, southerly-facing room Jay had handed over to her as a work-room, and set herself to work on the next season's designs, working like a dog worrying at a bone until her eyes were almost dropping out with the strain and her fingers cramped with cutting and sewing the fine, malleable fabrics she liked to work with. Then she would visit her mother, find time to take a long walk with Kit, and thoroughly whip herself into a miserable resentment by noticing how well the two of them were coming on under Jay's undeniable care.

But the nights were unavoidable, and Jay was always there, smiling at her, taunting her new escapist tactics with that amused glint in his eye. And the shutting of that bedroom door meant the night-long ravaging of her senses as Jay, with the kind of aching tenderness which flayed her vulnerable heart, wooed her—it was the only way she could describe it—wooed her with the sweet, sweet taste of his own passionate love.

They began arriving at around three, the first car turning in through the Lodge gates and making its way up the tree-lined driveway towards the house.

'Joe Tyndell will be the first to arrive, I see,' Jay murmured, watching with Rebecca from the drawing-room window as the dark blue four-wheel-drive Sierra pulled around the curve of the forecourt and stopped just in front of the house. 'This should be interesting,' he added with a touch of mocking humour. 'Come on,' he then commanded her before she could question just what that cryptic remark meant, taking her hand in his and threading it through the warm crook of his arm. 'It's time to show our united front. Kit?' he called to their son, who was engrossed in trying to look as relaxed as his father, when really he was perhaps as bothered as Rebecca was at the pending ordeal.

At least she knew she looked good, Rebecca consoled herself as, in a threesome, they moved into the hall to begin greeting their guests. Her dress was one of her own, made, during her long hours spent hiding from Jay in her studio, out of a piece of fine-textured black silk knit, high-necked, long-sleeved but subtly moulding her figure down to the neat rounded curves of her knee. Jay had taken one look at her and gleamed—that hot, sexy gleam which told her how much he was going to enjoy taking it off her later. And she'd had to bite into her inner lip to stop herself responding.

He looked good too in a pair of black silk mohair trousers which fitted smoothly against the flat of his hips and the long power of his legs, the open collar to his white silk shirt standing out in flattering contrast to the plain black V-neck sweater he wore over it; the ultimate lean moving machine, a man who could disturb women's senses just by their looking at him, whether he was trying to impress or not.

Kit was in black cords and a pale blue sweat-shirt, his face scrubbed clean, for once, and shining, while his unruly dark hair had been scraped into a kind of order for the occasion. He stood awkwardly at Jay's other side, watching, through lowered lids, Joe Tyndell, his wife and his little boy come in through the front door.

'Jay!' Joe came briskly forward to take his hand, his manner so obviously relaxed and friendly that Rebecca allowed herself a small smile, ruefully accepting that, far from being sworn enemies, these two men seemed to have become good friends—which only helped to puzzle her further, since Jay had once chosen to convince himself that she'd run away because of Joe.

'Well,' Joe turned to look at Rebecca, 'if it isn't our beautiful Becky, back home where she belongs at last!' That old roguish glint she used to love so much about him shone in his soft brown eyes and made her heart turn over in memory of its lethal charm.

'Hello, Joe,' she said a little reservedly, still suspicious of Jay's motives in asking Joe here today, and even more unsure just how destructive the rumours about them had been ten years ago; both Jay and her mother had referred to them, which could only mean that they had been common speculation in the area.

But Joe's smile was clear of any condemnation as he took her hand in a light grasp and raised it in a mocking salute halfway to his lips. And Rebecca found herself able to relax a little and return his warm smile.

Always a handsome man—he hadn't changed in that respect, she noted—Joe was big and broad, with a mop of pale golden hair and the fresh swarthy features of a man who spent ninety per cent of his life in the open air. As competition for Jay in their younger days, Joe was perhaps the only one to give Jay a running, in Rebecca's view.

'So, he got you tied to him at last,' he murmured mockingly, sending Jay one of his glinting looks.

'And intend to keep her that way,' Jay warned, 'so keep your roaming eye to yourself, Tyndell.'

'What's this about my husband having a roaming eye?' a sharp voice put in.

Jay laughed and gathered a tiny bundle of fluffy-haired blonde into his arms, kissing her wholeheartedly on her petal-soft cheek. 'What's sauce for the goose, Lyndsey, darling...' he murmured meaningfully.

'Lyndsey?' Eyes widening, Rebecca stared at the woman who until that moment had been completely hidden behind her big husband. She disentangled herself from Jay's warm embrace to turn a wry smile to Rebecca.

'The very same,' Lyndsey drily confirmed, 'but, if you don't mind, Becky, I would rather you kept your hands off my man this time around—he always did harbour a secret yen for you!'

Dark colour spread up Rebecca's cheeks, the censoriousness coming after she had just convinced herself she was worrying unnecessarily, sending her stepping back a pace into the protective curve of Jay's arm.

And her old friend from her schooldays suddenly looked stricken. 'Hell, Becky,' she cried, 'I didn't mean it that way!'

'My wife the mouth,' Joe drawled from behind her, and earned himself a frosty glare before Lyndsey was stepping up to grasp Rebecca by both hands.

'I didn't mean it in the literal sense, you idiot!' she scolded wretchedly. 'Good grief—Joe and Jay sorted all that out about you years ago!'

Had they? she thought with a bewildered blink.

'Before I married the fool, that's for sure,' Lyndsey confirmed. 'Or I wouldn't have walked down the street with him, never mind up the aisle as his wife!' She sent Joe a disdainful glance before turning her lovely green eyes back on Rebecca in abject appeal. 'It was a joke! That was all,' she explained. 'A joke!'

'But watch out, Rebecca,' Joe put in drily, 'her jokes are worse than her bite!'

'Oh, shut up, you!' his wife ordered him. 'God, I feel awful now!' she groaned at Rebecca. 'But I never thought you would even know about it all, never mind——'

'Rebecca, this is our son, Joe Junior,' Joe senior intervened, his tone sending the colour sweeping up his poor wife's cheeks. 'He, thank God, is a chip off the old block where I am concerned, and bears no resemblance at all to his outspoken mother!'

'I do so!' a stubborn voice protested, sending his father a look so like the one Lyndsey had sent him a moment earlier that Rebecca couldn't help it—she smiled. 'I'm just like Mummy—you're always saying so!'

'Did I forget to mention to you that this family are certified as the crazy nuts of this area?' Jay drawled close to her cheek. Rebecca turned her head to look pensively at him. But he was smiling with his eyes, no hint of accusation or aggression in him. 'Kit...' deftly he brought their shyly waiting son into things, his free hand clasped firmly on the boy's shoulder as he drew him closer to his other side '... these people are Mr and Mrs Tyndell, and their son Junior,' he introduced them, then finished proudly, 'Our son Kit.'

'Good grief.' gasped Lyndsey, staring at Kit. 'Talk about chips off the old block, Joe—this young man couldn't be anyone but Jay's son!'

'Thank you,' said Jay smilingly, then bent down to whisper in Kit's ear, 'This is where you do your bit, son,' promptingly.

After they had eyed each other awkwardly for a few seconds, Kit stepped forward and said to Junior in his politest voice, 'Would you like a drink of orange?'

'Orange—sure.' The other boy shrugged, and they both slouched off, uncomfortable in each other's company. Rebecca watched them go, the natural fears of a mother launching her offspring into a strange environment showing in the way her small white teeth pressed down on her bottom lip.

'It's all right, Becky...' It was Lyndsey who reassured her. 'We may be thought crazy around here, but we're a kind bunch. Give them five minutes and they'll be tearing around the place, tripping everyone up!'

'Yes, I'm sure you're right...' She turned anxious eyes on Lyndsey to find her studying her gravely, and smiled at last, a small natural smile.

'I really didn't mean to embarrass you before, you know. In fact, I've been looking forward to meeting you again after all these years, and——'

'Come on, Lyndsey,' a fond wrench on her arm brought Joe's tiny wife leaping back to his side, 'the others are arriving, and we're hogging the stars of the show, so nod nicely and move along, dear, like you've been taught to do at things like this...'

'I'm nodding—I'm nodding!' Lyndsey informed Joe tartly as they walked off together towards the cocktails already mixed and waiting to be tasted. 'I'll catch you later, Becky!' she called out over her shoulder. 'And we'll have a good talk...!'

'She was just like that at school,' Rebecca heard herself murmuring bewilderedly as she watched them walk away, still sniping at each other, yet with their arms closely entwined.

'No offence taken?' Jay asked lightly.

'No.' She looked up at him and smiled a little lop-sidedly. 'Well,' she said, 'maybe a little at first. Jay...' she then began awkwardly, '...about Joe and me——'

'Later, darling,' he cut in smoothly, his attention already smilingly fixed on the next clutch of people to arrive.

And her explanations had to wait, or, as she told herself a few minutes later, were perhaps fortunately curtailed before she made an utter fool of herself by trying to defend something which had never happened!

And her chin came up accordingly, that hint of proud challenge in her grey eyes helping her to get through the next hour, until all Jay's guests had arrived and been formally introduced to her—bar one, and the fact that Olivia had not yet put in an appearance played on Rebecca's nerves as, with Jay keeping her firmly by his side, they mingled with their guests, creating, as he had determined from the outset of this marriage, a united front to all who wished to challenge them.

Some people she recognised from ten years ago, some she did not. And she found, as she mingled through the little groups, chatting shyly to them, that she could see why Jay had invited them. They were all warm and friendly people, pleasantly eager to make her feel welcome into their selective group, if only for Jay's sake.

It took Olivia's arrival to cast a shadow over things. And, not for the first time, Rebecca found herself wondering why Jay had invited her when it was obvious that everyone else present felt just as uncomfortable as Rebecca did having her there, their faces stiffening up, and hooded questioning glances passing from one guest to another.

She turned up wearing the most exquisite couture silk suit in a soft peach to match her perfect skin, pausing in the open doorway to the drawing-room, calmly waiting for everyone to notice her, and it was only by Olivia's slight lifting of her small chin as she watched all those eyes turn on her that Rebecca realised how much she was having to ask of herself to come here today, as Jay's long-term lover, to meet Rebecca for the first time as his legal wife.

She had come here as the loser, and there wasn't a person present in the room who was not aware of it. Yet her chin stayed high, her poise calm, and when she finally allowed her gaze to settle on Rebecca and Jay she managed to come forward with a smiling grace, offering them her best wishes without even sounding bitter.

'That's my girl,' Jay murmured sardonically as she moved away from them, his narrowed gaze fixed on her sensuously swaying figure. 'Show them all you don't give a damn.'

'Oh, don't be so sarcastic!' Rebecca whispered crossly. 'It has to have been hard for her coming here. And I can't say it has been easy for me, having you flaunt your ex-mistress in front of me!'

'*Ex-what?*' he drawled, then grinned at the astounded look he'd managed to put on Rebecca's face before, with a mocking brush of his lips against her stiff cheek, he strolled away, going to check on the children who were ensconced in the back sitting-room where the furniture had been cleared and a selection of different games provided to keep them happy, while she stared dumbly after him, knowing herself to have been completely and thoroughly put down.

Yet, even while she seethed in silence, wanting to rush after him and demand he explain that last remark, her eyes were busily eating him up, taking in the lithe grace with which he moved, the long, lean, harshly powered sexuality of his body which made that mantle of urbane sophistication he carried around with him such a damned lie. Jay was all male animal, possessive, territorial, and primitive.

'Watch it—your heart is showing,' a dry voice murmured just beside her, and Rebecca swung around to find Lyndsey smiling at her. 'Put it away,' she advised mock-solemnly. 'There are one or two bitches here who might fancy putting a knife in it if you keep it on show.' Then, with her lovely eyes clouding into seriousness, 'Forgive the outspokenness again, Becky, but our dear Olivia means trouble. She always has and she always will where Jay is concerned. She's considered him her exclusive property for as far back as I can remember, and I can't really see your being married to him now changing that opinion by one iota!'

A feeling began to churn deep inside her, and Rebecca stood for a moment, trying to contain it, knowing what it was and hating herself for feeling it, but unable to stop it surging hotly inside her. It was jealousy and possessiveness and a deep damning fury for the man she was married to for allowing Olivia even a moment's encouragement by inviting her here today!

Obviously Jay enjoyed having his women at his feet, she thought angrily, and made a firm decision to never let him get her there again!

'Hey—what's this about your being Salamander, by the way?' Lyndsey's awed tone dismissed the subject of Olivia to bring Rebecca's mind back to the present and her social smile back to her face.

'Shocking, isn't it,' she mocked herself drily, 'that little Becky Shaw should have turned out so successful?'

'Damned amazing, if you ask me!' Lyndsey said bluntly. 'At school you hated even applying a thread to needle!' she reminded her scornfully. 'So how come you're now making a fortune doing just that?'

'Necessity,' she sighed, her eyes clouding for a moment when she recalled those early years when any job which brought in some extra cash had been more than welcome to her. 'Sheer necessity. I needed the money, and the only thing I could do from home while Kit was tiny was sew. Don't forget that, hate it or not, I used to have to help my mother sew and mend here when I was younger.' Her eyes made a bleak scan of the lovely cream and bitter-lemon drawing-room, remembering the times she had sat here for hours, painstakingly repairing a worn hem on the heavy damask curtains, or placing tiny blind patches in antique linen and lace. Wild and reckless she might have been, but she had had her chores to do too, in the times when the art of patience and a pride in neat sewing had been drummed into her from a very early age.

'Is that a Salamander?' Lyndsey was eyeing Rebecca's black dress with open envy.

'Want to see the label?' She grinned, then confessed, 'Actually, I made this up only this week. It's an old design, but one which comes back on to the rail year after year because of its clean, classical lines.'

'Classical it may be,' Lyndsey drawled, 'but the cut does something pretty spectacular to your figure.'

'Thank you.' Rebecca laughed, sounding so natural for the first time that several people turned to gaze in her direction, Jay being one of them and Olivia another, both with their eyes narrowed and assessing. 'I could make you one, if you would like me to?' she offered Lyndsey.

The blue eyes widened. 'Me?' she choked. 'I can't afford a Salamander!' she scoffed at the offer. 'Not on a farmer's pay, I can't. No,' she refused, looking frankly envious, 'the designer life is not for me—which is a downright crime in my opinion since I have trouble finding anything to fit my stupid, tiny frame!' she complained. 'Everything is either too long, or too wide, or——'

'Too everything,' Rebecca finished for her with a sympathy and understanding which came from years of dealing with women whose size and shape were not in the ordinary run of things. 'But seriously, Lyndsey,' already her designer mind was running over her friend's petite figure, covering it in soft, flowing fabrics, shaping them, moulding them into something to suit the woman's pearly skin and fine-boned shape, 'I have the most delicious silk velvet elastin upstairs in my studio which would look spectacular on you.'

'But I can't afford you, Rebecca!' Lyndsey repeated sighingly.

'What's in a label?' Rebecca dismissed, grey eyes contemptuous. 'It's only a thin scrap of silk, after all, that costs me three pounds twenty pence to buy. I'll make you a dress for the price of the fabric, and you can buy a Salamander label off me as an added extra, if you want one.'

'Is that legal?' Lyndsey's eyes were popping out of her head.

Rebecca cocked an arching brow at her. 'I am Salamander!' she announced. 'I can do what the hell I want with my labels!'

They both fell into companionable laughter, and once again the room turned to stare: two lovely young women thoroughly enjoying each other's company. Jay smiled, satisfied, and turned away just in time to catch Olivia's seething glare on Rebecca, and the assessing look came back into his eyes.

'What would you prefer,' Rebecca went on temptingly, her grey eyes glinting with fun, 'something very suave and sophisticated which would make you look like a duchess, or something soft and slinky and very, very sexy which would knock Joe's eyes out?'

'Oh,' Lyndsey pouted, 'let's knock Joe's eyes out,' she decided instantly. 'It's something I've always wanted to do, after all.'

'Then...' she gave a quick glance around the crowded drawing-room, then turned a conspiratorial look on Lyndsey which sent the other girl flinging back through the years to when that kind of expression had only meant trouble for the pair of them '...let's slip away right now and take a quick look at some designs in my studio—we can be back down here before anyone even misses us.'

Ten minutes later they came back down the stairs, giggling mischievously together, the design and fabric Rebecca had come up with for Lyndsey so disgustingly sexy that the tiny blonde actually blushed. 'Knock his eyes out!' she gasped. 'If he had a suspect heart it would see him off, poor dear!'

'What have you two been up to to put those looks on your lovely faces, hmm?' a deep voice asked, and they both started guiltily, blushing when they found Joe standing watching them with a golden eyebrow raised in sardonic enquiry.

'What do you think we've been up to?' his wife demanded innocently. 'What do all ladies do when they disappear for a short while? We've been powdering our pretty little noses to make ourselves look more beautiful for you chauvinistic men!'

'Henpecked men, more like,' Joe mocked, then took a firm grip on his wife's arm and added drily, 'You're doing it again, darling,' he informed her wearily. 'Monopolising the star!'

'I know—I know...nod and move on, nod and move on...' she sighed, sending Rebecca a 'who'd have a bossy man?' look over her shoulder as she was pulled away.

Rebecca laughed softly as she watched them go, feeling more at home now than she had done since coming back to Thornley. She and Lyndsey had been close friends at school. And it was nice to find that the years hadn't changed their old childhood liking for being together. It made her feel warm inside, and reluctantly grateful to Jay for bringing this meeting about. For she was suddenly sure that he had done it for this purpose only, and not for the intention of seeing how she and Joe reacted towards each other.

The acceptance of that lifted her heart, and she was still smiling as she turned and walked off towards the ornately carved plaster archway which separated the front from the back of the house, her intention being to go and check on the children's play-room. But she had only just stepped into the shadows of the rear hall when the sound of voices coming from Jay's study had her standing still before she slowly changed direction and went to stand outside the slightly ajar door.

And what she heard made her go cold inside.

'When did it click with her that I never posted her wretched letter?'

It was Olivia's voice, sounding coarsely derisive.

CHAPTER THIRTEEN

'THAT really doesn't matter, does it?' Jay's voice came, quiet and cold, through the narrow gap in the door. 'The fact is that you lied and cheated your way into making my father conspire with you against us!'

'Lied to him?' Olivia's voice sounded shrill with scorn. 'It didn't take much, Jay,' she derided him. 'In fact, he was as damned eager as I was to find an excuse to kick her right out of your life! God!' she laughed. 'That letter, when I showed it to him, frightened the life out of him! He almost fell on me in gratitude when I told him what a cheap little trollop she was, and how there was no chance she could even know whose baby it was she was carrying!'

Feeling the cloying waves of sickness wash over her, Rebecca swayed, her eyes closing as she leaned heavily back against the wall.

'You ruined Rebecca's life—ruined my life—and even had a go at ruining Joe Tyndell's life just to get your own way! Yet what did you get out of it? What did you really? Ten years of frustration is what you got,' he answered his own question, hard and derisively. 'Ten years of trying every way you could think of to get me to fall into your bed, when all you had to do was ask me why I wouldn't so much as touch you and I would have told you the truth and saved us both a lot of heartache.'

'You wanted me once, Jay,' Olivia threw back bitterly. 'While you were tossing the little peasant in the hay, you hankered after a bit of class that summer— which was why you were always around at *my* home, lazing around *my* pool, admiring *my* body!'

'You really are a pathetic creature, Olivia,' Jay said witheringly. 'I wasn't there because of you!' he jeered. 'I was there because that was where Rebecca was! And if it meant having to put up with your self-centred and shallow company then I was prepared to do it—just so I knew I was keeping that vile little tongue of yours from cutting into her!'

'That's not true!'

'I go there because I know you're there!' he had said. Rebecca swallowed, knowing in that cold dizzying moment that it was true.

'That's not true, Jay!' Olivia insisted thickly. 'We were always meant for each other! God!' she choked. 'Don't you realise how your father will be turning in his grave because you've dared to bring her back here?'

'No,' Jay denied. 'My father hated the person you made Rebecca out to be. I know he was stern, and I know he was old-fashioned in his ideas about the social classes. But Rebecca had grown up on this estate. He was used to seeing her here. Had even grown quite fond of her in his own way. No...' Rebecca leaned weakly against the wall, her heart pounding against her clenched chest, imagining Jay's dark head shaking grimly '... it was the way you persuaded him to believe she was betraying me which made him act the way he did.'

'By giving her money to get rid of her child?' Olivia scoffed. 'That doesn't sound like an act of fondness in my books. It sounds like sheer damned horror to me!'

'Not just any child, Olivia,' Jay came back, his voice so cool and calm all the way through that it made Olivia's sound more shrill and coarse the longer this confrontation went on, 'but Joe Tyndell's child—as you put it— being foisted upon his own son. That was what he couldn't condone. And, although *I* can't condone the methods he used to protect me, I can at least understand them. Whereas your involvement has no excuse, has it? Simply being the malicious determination of a calculating and self-obsessed bitch!'

A short, telling silence followed Jay's cutting opinion of Olivia's character, then, 'My God...' she breathed. 'You're ready to absolve everyone from blame except for me, aren't you? I have to carry it all because it's the only way you can live with what your family did to her—when really, Jay, it is only by pure fluke that that boy is yours! No matter what Rebecca or Joe Tyndell told you, they were in each other's arms the moment your back was turned!'

Rebecca shot away from the wall, her eyes opening on a surge of blind fury that had her twisting around with the intention of going in there and——

'No.' A hand coming firm upon her arm stopped her, and she spun around to find Joe standing there, his swarthy face tight with anger. 'Let them finish,' he said quietly. 'Jay knows what he's doing. Let them finish.'

She heard Jay laugh then, the sound so harsh and cutting that it made her flinch, and Joe drew her trembling body back, holding her there with his hands firm on her arms as Jay murmured, drily, 'I'd like to hear you repeat that in front of Joe and his wife. Lyndsey is made of sterner stuff than Rebecca is—she'd yank your lying tongue out, then stand there happily watching you bleed to death!'

Joe laughed, just a soft huff of a sound deep in his chest, but Rebecca knew he was appreciating Jay's sardonic view of his wife.

'Why don't you just accept, Olivia,' he went on smoothly, 'that your dirty game has been exposed and it's time to back out graciously? I did warn you when I invited you here today,' he went on to remind her, 'that I was not prepared to take this kind of confrontation.'

'No...' she murmured shakily, 'you wanted your pound of flesh without it, didn't you? You really are a ruthless bastard, Jay,' she went on huskily. 'Setting this little gathering up—setting me up so that both they and I would get the message that, as far as you were concerned, I was no longer considered fit to know.'

'At last you seemed to have got the message,' Jay drawled without a modicum of human sympathy.

'Not one of them came down in support of me, did they?' At last Olivia was beginning to sound strained and beaten.

'You had it coming, Olivia,' Jay told her flatly. 'For ten long, bloody years you've had it coming. And now you've got it.'

'And all because she found out somehow about my not posting her blasted letter!' Olivia laughed a little wildly. 'It really is a kind of justice, isn't it, Jay? Because, you know, when I took that letter from Rebecca that day I was actually being kind! A rare thing for me, I do admit. It was only when I read the address and who it was going to that I decided not to bother. My,' she taunted drily, 'but it made an exciting read!'

Rebecca swayed again, the feeling of sickness draining the colour from her skin, and Joe held on to her, while in her mind's eye she was seeing that scene again, the one in which Olivia had climbed out of her black Mini into the pouring rain, looking for the moment when the distinctive blue envelope had to have slid from the mouth of the post-box and out again. Then she saw it, in the way Olivia had waved to her with her other hand high above her head, drawing Rebecca's eyes upwards as the hand holding the letter had slid smoothly into the pocket of Olivia's raincoat.

'Come on,' Joe said gruffly. 'I think you've heard enough.'

She nodded, too numbed inside to do much more than let him lead her away towards the shadows of the archway, where he paused, turning her to face him, his hands gentle on her trembling shoulders. It took her a moment, but she managed to lift her eyes to his.

'How much of that did you overhear?' she asked him huskily.

'Most of it.' He grimaced, then said questioningly, 'How much of it did you already know?'

Rebecca smiled emptily. 'Most of it,' she threw back drily, thinking, all but the most important part. The part which told her that Jay had never received her letter. She shuddered, and Joe's grip on her tightened in concern.

'I saw them go into Jay's study together just before you and Lyndsey came downstairs,' he explained his reason for being there. 'And I thought something like this might happen when I saw you walk off towards this part of the house, so I deposited Lyndsey with the Crowthers then came back to try and head you off, only it was too late.' His smile was wry. 'She's been angling after getting him alone since she arrived,' he went on flatly. 'Everyone knew it—including Jay. But not everyone knew the reasons why she wanted to get him alone.' He turned his sombre brown eyes on her. 'She's been behaving a little desperately ever since you arrived back on the scene,' he said grimly. 'The fact that Jay then locked you all away here at the Hall only made her worse. Everyone in the crowd had noticed it, worried about her because it has always been so obvious that she was madly obsessed with Jay. When he married you it left her with nothing—nothing, do you understand?' Rebecca nodded bleakly, knowing just how that felt. 'But what I hadn't realised was how cancerous that obsession was, Becky—until I heard all that just now.' He turned his face away for a moment, his solid jaw clenching with anger and distaste. 'I thought that incident ten years ago had made my life bloody difficult, but it bears no comparison to what it did to you, does it? God,' he said tightly, 'when I think how that bitch——!' He stopped, sighing harshly. 'Are you going to be all right?' he asked her. 'Shall I go and break that scene up and get Jay for you?'

'No.' She shook her head, not wanting to come face to face with Jay just yet. She wasn't ready. She had too much painful thinking to do. 'I—I had better get back to our other guests,' she murmured distractedly, moving away from him—then turned back to look sombrely at him. 'I seem to have unknowingly caused you a lot of grief, Joe. I hope you learned to forgive me at some time.'

His smile was tight with protest. 'I never blamed you for any of it, Becky, only resented the way people were so quick to link our names together when you disappeared as you did. Now I know why...' He sighed, the anger burning bright in his eyes. 'She must have spread those stories about. As I said, I suspected at the time that it might have been Olivia who—but...well...' He shrugged his broad shoulders, too angry and disgusted to want to go on. 'The woman is like a cancer. It makes me sick inside to know I actually used to count her as one of my friends.'

At around six, people began to drift away, smiling, offering return invitations, complimenting both Jay and Rebecca on their pleasant-mannered son, and in general announcing their desire to extend these first links they had tied with Jay's new family. Rebecca hadn't seen Olivia leave, but she had seen Jay come back into the drawing-room only a few minutes after she had done herself.

His eyes had sought her out, the blue still glinting with the residue of his anger. Her heart had lurched, the shocking realisation that she had misjudged him so badly for all this time cutting into her like a knife set jaggedly into her soul, and she had had to turn away from him, begin chatting lightly to the people close to her, pretending nothing was wrong, that everything in her world was rosy, when she was being torn apart inside by the terrible pangs of a guilt it was her turn to feel.

It had been only a few minutes later that he had joined her, his arm coming warm about her waist, and he'd drawn her into his side, his dark head lowering so he could place his lips against her cold pale cheek. 'I love you,' he'd murmured, and she hadn't been able to bear it, the horror of it all sending her twisting around to face him, her grey eyes bright with anguish.

'Jay——' she'd murmured thickly.

'Later,' he'd said. And it was then that she'd seen it—the knowledge like a dark burn in his eyes. He knew she had overheard. Joe must have told him.

The last of the stragglers departed, and they waved them goodbye with their bright social smiles pinned to their faces while they throbbed with a multitude of emotions beneath. Jay held her loosely clamped beneath his arm, and Kit stood beside her, looking flushed and happy, still riding high on the success of his afternoon. He had found three other boys here today who would be in the same class as he when he started school next term, had received invitations from all and sundry to go and play, and, looking down at him, Rebecca wanted to weep for everything he had lost during the last ten years.

As soon as they were alone Rebecca excused herself, mumbling something about popping upstairs and leaving Jay to contend with their son's excited chatter. It was a good half-hour before he came looking for her, and found her standing in the long window of their bedroom, the heavy curtain drawn back so that she could gaze out on the crisp starlit night.

He paused to study her slender body framed in the darkness of the window, before closing the door and coming to stand beside her. She was hugging herself as if cold, her grey eyes bleak as together they watched the full moon edge its way over a cloudless sky.

'There's going to be a hard frost tonight,' she said quietly.

'Mmm,' he murmured in absent agreement. Then huskily, 'Becky, love...'

Rebecca turned to look at him. 'How did you find out about the letter?'

He shoved his hands into his trouser pockets, grimacing at the way she had come directly to the point. 'It had been really puzzling me, that,' he told her. 'How my letter must have got into my father's hands instead of my own. I wondered at first if, in your anxiety, you'd put the wrong address on the damned thing, then dismissed that idea as downright escapism from the real bloody point of it all, which was that my father—my own damned father,' he repeated painfully, 'had plotted something so unforgivable against his own flesh and blood!' He sucked in a tight breath of air, then let it out again, his lean face drawn with the bitter disillusionment that knowledge filled him with.

'When you told me about your interview with my father,' he continued after a moment, 'so many little things began to niggle at my mind—like his furious attitude to my coming home early from America for instance . . .'

'You came back before your year was up?' she asked in surprise.

Jay sent her a grim look. 'I was back here within two damned months!' he growled, moving restlessly away from her as though the memories of that time still had the ability to haunt him. 'What did you expect me to do when I hadn't heard a single word from you since I arrived there? You promised to write to me every week! I received not one rotten word from you, and I was going out of my mind missing you, worrying about you! You were so damned young and impulsive!' He groaned. 'Anything could have happened! I rang the house and asked them to put your mother on so I could find out if anything was wrong, but she was always unavailable. My father was no more forthcoming. "Becky?" he'd say as if he had to really think to know who I was talking about. "She's got a job somewhere as far as I know—ask her mother." And I was fobbed off like that for weeks before it really began to hit me that something desperate had to be wrong! I caught the next plane home and faced my father with the fact that I was in love with you and wanted to marry you before I went back to America. He almost had a seizure on the spot! Called you some pretty sick names, for which I hit him, for the first time in my damned life, then I walked out! Went back to the Lodge to face your mother again...'

'Back to the Lodge?' she murmured in confusion, having to concentrate to take all of this in.

He nodded curtly. 'I'd already stopped there on my way to demand to see you. Your mother told me you weren't home so I asked where you were and how long you would be. She went all shifty on me, giving me non-answers which made no damned sense whatsoever, so I told her I'd come back later, and decided to go and face my father, so that when I did eventually find you I could at least have some kind of excuse to offer you for racing back home like a demented fool! I had my pride too, you know!' he answered the wide bewildered look she gave him. 'For all I knew you could have been off with anyone—you certainly hadn't bothered to write to me— and I could have been walking into egg on my face.'

'So they eventually told you I'd run away to have Joe's baby aborted, and you naturally believed it!' she grimly assumed.

'No, I damned well did not!' he denied, throwing her a bitter look. 'I am not a fool, you know, Rebecca, though I've behaved like one over you for the best part of my life!' He sighed, sighed again, then shook himself impatiently. 'I was still sane enough then to know—if only by the arithmetic of it!—that, if you were pregnant, then it was with my child! And, God knows, I've never felt so bloody awful in my life as I did then, knowing I'd left you to cope alone, probably frightened, ob- viously cast out, if your mother's refusal to even talk about you was anything to go by. And I went through the worst months of my life then, trying to find you. Worrying about you, certain you would not do anything to harm our child. Yet,' he added wearily, 'as the weeks went by, then the months, and I still hadn't a clue where you were, I began to believe it,' he admitted. 'For my own sanity's sake,' he explained, 'or I don't think I could have lived with my own sense of guilt.'

'Oh, Jay!' she whispered, moving to drop down weakly on the edge of the bed when her trembling legs at last gave out beneath her, her face blanched white with the horror of it all. 'I'm so sorry!' He'd gone through hell for her, and she'd believed him capable of rejecting her and Kit!

'You're sorry?' he ground out, staring at her as if she'd gone mad. 'How the hell do you think I've been feeling since I found out about Kit?' He stalked over to the bed, then turned to look down at her, the pain of it all stark on his tense face. 'It's been eating me up inside knowing how hard you've had it over the last ten years, gleaning from bits Kit has said when he's innocently described something from his early childhood which told me how difficult it was for you both. And when you told me about that damned letter...' He stopped, swallowing, taking in a deep breath to try to contain the bitter emotions raging inside him.

Rebecca said huskily, 'I wrote it just a week after you left, Jay. It was the first and only letter I ever sent you.'

'And my father faced you with my reply,' he concluded grimly. Rebecca lowered her eyes from him, the pain of that meeting still able to hurt her. 'Your mother told me only last week about her own interview with him. She was glad, I think, to get the whole thing off her chest. She's been living with the guilt of her part in your betrayal too long. God knows,' he sighed a little tragically, 'I would like to believe that my own father felt some sense of guilt, but I will never be sure. Certainly as the months went by and I refused to have anything to do with him or his precious company, he had to be regretting something, because he came around to see me where I was staying in Harrogate and asked me to forgive him. I thought he was asking forgiveness for the way he'd insulted you in front of me, but perhaps it was for more than that.' He drew a wretched hand through his hair. 'I went back to work for him,' he went on heavily, 'but only because I didn't really care what I

did by then. I felt so damned betrayed by you, Rebecca!'
he whispered unsteadily. 'So damned betrayed——'

'Don't.' The emotion throbbing in his voice sent her
up off the bed and over to him, her arms winding tightly
around his lean, hard frame, feeling the shudders rack
him, the awful after-waves of ten bleak years.

'Then there you were,' he murmured suddenly, his
voice gone soft and rueful, 'my Rebecca, ten years on,
walking towards me like a dream right out of my lonely
nights, and I didn't know whether I wanted to kill you
or hug you, you looked so damned beautiful!' A sigh
ripped through him, rasping in the deep, tense cavern
of his chest beneath her resting cheek. 'And there was
Olivia that same night,' he went on darkly. 'Still in my
life, sitting at my table, eating my food—and slyly re-
minding me, after you'd left us alone, of the rumours
about you and Joe, and how I'd gone around to his farm
to beat the living daylights out of him. God!' He shuddered. 'How I hate that woman! When I think of all the
lies she's told—she's the one who told me you'd gone
off to abort Joe's child in the first place!' he ground out
thickly. 'She's the one who therefore sent me hot-footing
it round there to thump the damned truth out of him!'

'And did you?' She raised her head to look curiously
at him. 'Did you thump poor Joe?'

'Several times,' he drawled and Rebecca saw the rueful
smile of reminiscence touch his angry mouth. 'And got
pretty well thumped back in return,' he admitted. 'By
the time we both fell into a breathless heap on the ground
I'd calmed down enough to listen, and Joe was too
damned exhausted to be bothered to lie. You can tell
sometimes when someone is telling you the truth,' he
added thoughtfully. 'It's like a sixth sense which switches
on to give a positive light, and it wasn't as though I
wanted to mistrust you, it was just that I think I wanted
Joe's confirmation that you hadn't turned straight to
him from me.'

'Yes.' Rebecca quietly understood; she'd felt that same instinctive pull herself when Jay had repeatedly denied all knowledge of her letter—only, instead of wanting to trust his word, she'd forced herself not to. Because it had meant too much to dare.

'It was Joe who told me what a vicious little cat Olivia was, that he suspected it was she who had been spreading the filthy rumour that he was supposed to have got you pregnant. He was damned furious, I can tell you, cursing you for disappearing so you couldn't clear his name, cursing me for being fool enough to get you pregnant—if you were at all, which both of us at that point began to doubt—and threatening to murder Olivia because she'd messed up his life with Lyndsey, who refused to even speak to him.'

'Very interesting,' Rebecca drawled, lifting her cheek from its warm place next to his heart to look up at him, 'but there wasn't a single thing in all that which actually points the finger of suspicion for my missing letter in Olivia's way.'

'No, there wasn't, was there?' he agreed, smiling a little as he ran his possessive eyes over her upturned face. His hand came up to stroke her hair, pinned still in its neat, tight knot. 'I asked Christina,' he said simply. 'I rang her up and asked her if she would do me the favour of telling me everything she knew about what had happened ten years ago, and she took great pleasure in relaying the lot, cuttingly and accusingly, with hardly a breath taken in between, then sat back on the other end of the phone and waited for me to defend myself. I did,' he informed Rebecca, 'most adequately, I may add. But you had insisted we did not talk about the past at all, and,' he sighed, 'I was willing to accept you had a right to expect me to prove myself to you again without any excuses to help me, which I was prepared to do—and have enjoyed the challenge in the meantime.' His eyes gleamed wicked thoughts at her, and Rebecca blushed under their teasing light. 'But,' he went on without remorse, 'Olivia asked for all she got today, Rebecca. She'd already begun more rumours about you among my friends, using their lack of knowledge about our relationship ten years ago as a base for her poisoned darts. Calling Kit the result of a one-night stand——' His mouth snapped shut, lips thinned and clenched against the sudden burst of anger that welled inside him. 'Joe called me up to warn me that it was all starting again, and that's when I decided to get to the bottom of it, once and for all. So I went to see your mother on my own during one of my brief trips into the office, and, although she couldn't really add anything to what you'd already told me on that God-awful night at your home, she did mumble something about Olivia's coming to the Hall, demanding to see my father, on the same day he had had you hauled up in front of him. It set a little seed of suspicion growing in my mind. And a couple of days later I rang Christina, grasping at straws really.' He grimaced. 'But then I heard her story about Olivia's posting your letter for you, and her candid opinion that, whoever this Olivia was, she was a bitch of the first order and shouldn't be let near you if I had any sense at all, and that was when it all fell neatly into place,' he finished heavily. 'It had to have been Olivia who'd kept your letter and given it to my father. The rest I worked out from a few long hours of sitting whipping myself into a fury in my study.'

'The day you decided to put on this little party we had today,' Rebecca concluded, remembering his mood for the rest of that day.

'The day I decided to tell you unequivocally that I still loved you,' he reminded her huskily. 'You deserved that, my darling, no matter whether you scoffed me out of the room or not. You deserved to hear those words. I owed them to you for ten long years of excommunication for my sins, not yours.'

'Oh, Jay!' she sighed, hating the ugliness of it all, and buried her face in his jumper once again, needing the comfort of his big solid presence.

'But I did not set up today's little shindig to open your eyes to the truth, Becky,' he then went on grimly. 'I did it to make sure Olivia and all my friends knew just where my allegiance lies, by dropping a subtle hint here and there so she would know I was now aware of what she'd done, and dropping other just as subtle hints around the gathering to the effect that Olivia was no longer considered a friend of this family—which then left them all with the decision of whom they preferred to keep friendly with. They chose us,' he announced with the glib arrogance of one who had already known the outcome. 'And, in consequence, Olivia would have got her come-uppance at their hands. Not mine. She was supposed to then leave quietly with her head bowed in defeat. But she didn't.' His hard mouth thinned, the anger returning when he recalled the ugly scene in his study. 'In typical style, I suppose, for one who's usually managed to worm her way out of most things, she decided to confront me with it all in the hope that she would set her nasty little schemes moving again.'

'The cold premeditation of it all!' Rebecca shivered, and Jay's arms closed more tightly around her. 'It's frightening to know that other people can get such a tight control over how we act or what we believe,' she murmured bleakly, shivering again, 'yet she must love you badly to have gone to such extremes to part us.'

'Not love,' Jay denied, 'but obsession. Olivia was obsessed with the idea of me, an idea encouraged by my father and strengthened by a natural envy of what you and I shared. Don't feel sorry for her, Rebecca,' he warned grimly. 'She doesn't deserve it. Nor my father, come to that,' he added bleakly, 'or he would have at least tried to confess his sins to me before he died...'

'Or maybe, as you said to Olivia, he actually believed the lies she fed to him,' she suggested, preferring to believe Jay's version of his father's part in it all, rather than the black, hating one she'd carried around with her for so many years.

'You're far more forgiving than I am if you can make yourself believe that,' he said grimly.

'If I can forgive my mother her part in it all, Jay,' Rebecca said quietly, 'I can forgive your father his—after all,' she lifted her face to smile with a glint of her old mischief alight in her eyes, 'he did give me five thousand pounds to go away with! It was almost worth all the trouble just to have that much money!'

'You mercenary little she-devil!' Jay scolded, beginning to smile himself, then his eyes darkened and he reached up to cup her soft cheek with his hand. 'You're a beautiful person, Rebecca Lorence. Beautiful, inside and out, and I shall go on loving you till the end of my days—and beyond.'

He kissed her then, for the first time in ten long years bringing their mouths to meet in a true honesty, and Rebecca felt her heart swell as all the warmth and love she'd held so tightly suppressed inside it burst joyously free.

'You know what?' Jay said suddenly, drawing his warm lips across her cheek to bury them in the sensitive hollow by her lobe. 'I have this—uncontrollable urge to take a walk down by the river.'

'Now?' Rebecca lifted her head to stare at him, and immediately saw his intention written in the burning glow of his eyes. 'You have to be joking!' she protested, already feeling the stinging beginnings of her own desire uncoiling to meet with his. 'It's below freezing out there!'

'Are you questioning my ability to keep you warm?' he drawled. The sting became a burn as he drew his hands sensuously down her back to meet at her soft behind.

'Where's that old Rebecca love for the different gone, hmm?' he challenged softly.

'It's still here,' she whispered. Then, as the wretched tears of all the pain and heartache they had gone through filled her eyes, and she flung her arms around his neck, 'Oh, Jay!' she choked out achingly, 'I do l——'

'No,' he cut in, covering her mouth with his fingers. 'Don't say it. Not now, but there, when we're by the river. Back where you first said it to me. Tell me there, Becky,' he urged her fiercely. 'I want to hear you say it there!'

CHAPTER FOURTEEN

THE moon slid on a lazy trail across the star-kissed sky. The river turned silver beneath its colourless glow. The ground felt hard and frosty as Rebecca slid her arms above her head and stretched sensuously up to reach for the moon.

Jay stood, as naked as she, several feet away, the cold striking at his flesh without his being aware of it. Watching her, he held his body in taut suspension as his Rebecca came alive again in front of his hungry eyes. Behind him lay the pile of clothes he had hastily discarded, both his and hers, before she'd slipped teasingly away from him to go and stand alone in the centre of the clearing, putting on this alluring display for him alone.

Her hair flowed dark and glistening down her back, her breasts, dark-tipped and full, shone like pearls in the moonlight, her slender body arched and inviting, lovely face softened into that old remembered expression of wanton woman.

'Well,' she murmured as she relaxed back into a pose of provocative temptation, her grey eyes glinting challenge and demand at him from beneath the seductive weight of her dark lashes, 'what are you waiting for?'

His chest rose and fell on a shaken sigh, his jaw held tight against the pounding tension in his body. 'You know what,' he said, not attempting to close the gap between them. 'You know what I'm waiting for, you damned, tormenting little witch!'

She smiled, teasing him with the soft upward curve of her lips, her body, sheathed in silver light. *'No!'* she refused, and turned, balancing lightly on the slender balls of her feet as she made ready to flee.

Jay caught her by the flying pelt of her hair, twisting her around so he could see the shining triumph in her laughing, taunting face. Anger whipped across his, and his body came hard against her own, already hardened with passion, already eager to bury itself in the warm luxury of her flesh.

She laughed out loud, exalting in his anger, the sound ringing out in the dark night sky.

'God in heaven,' he muttered hoarsely, and caught her mouth with his own.

And there in the silvered light of their special clearing, he swung her away on a journey back through the years to a time when coming here meant everything to their love-crazed souls.

He joined with her, bracing her to him with hands cupping the small neat curve of her thighs while her arms clung to his neck, head thrown back, lips parted and eyes lost in the exquisite delirium which was Jay.

'I love you,' she kept on chanting at him. 'I love you, I love you, I love you...'

'I know it,' he threw harshly back at her, 'I've always known it! I shall always know it, you foolish, adorable—beautiful witch!'

'Always, Jay?' she murmured later, when they stood leaning against the hard bark of a winter-shorn maple tree, kissing gently, stroking, softly touching each other with the tenderness which should always follow the rage of loving.

'Always,' he nodded confidently. 'Even while you hated me it was a kind of love I recognised, because I felt the same way myself. Hurt, wounded even, most definitely afraid of letting the true feelings come through again. But it was love, Rebecca,' he stated certainly. 'Love all the way—how could it not be with the way we've always felt about each other?'

'I'm sorry I didn't believe you about the letter,' she sighed, reaching up to catch his lobe between her lips, and sucking delicately on it.

He shuddered. 'I couldn't have expected you to, darling,' he said, clearing her of all blame. 'It was so obvious to me that you were sure of your facts. And I knew, from the moment that you told me about my father's part in it all, that it was I who had to prove myself worthy of your love, and not the other way around.'

'But all those wasted years, Jay...' She moved wretchedly in front of him.

'Forget them,' he commanded. 'They're gone, and pining for what we lost can only spoil what we have to come, so forget them, Rebecca, put them out of your mind. We made it through in the end, and really that's all that matters.'

'Yes,' she breathed, then frowned at him. 'You're freezing,' she told him in concern, her hands trailing down his cold, shivering flesh, then she smiled up at him, her grey eyes overflowing with love. 'Let's go home, Jay,' she said softly. 'I want Kit to share in all this wonderful love we've found again.'

Jay nodded his dark head and looked at her through dark, intense eyes. 'You don't know how good that sounds to me, darling, having you call my house your home at last.'

Walking into the house some time later, their arms wrapped possessively around each other, they caught Kit just coming downstairs and about to make for the kitchen. He stopped when he saw them and frowned.

'What's the matter with you two?' he asked curiously. 'You look—different.'

'We're in love with each other,' Jay said simply.

'Oh, is that all?' Kit scoffed, and continued on his way towards the kitchen, calling over his shoulder, 'I thought you'd won the pools at least, by the silly looks on your faces!'

'So much for sharing it all with him!' Rebecca said deflatedly.

'Never mind, darling,' Jay soothed. 'Share it with me—I always was your most devoted fan, after all!'

She laughed, and reached up to kiss him. 'Hmm,' she murmured against his warm lips. 'I suppose you'll have to do... Yes...I suppose you will...'